Duplicitous

by Marty Smith

This book is dedicated to my mother Margaretta Smith, who was always in the middle of a good novel no matter how busy she was raising all of us kids and saving her own small corner of the world.

Chapter 1

A steady rain was falling. I sat staring at my windshield, watching raindrops splatter and form thin rivulets that zigzagged down the glass. Periodically the windshield wipers swept it away and I could see the brownstone building across the street with a large stone arch over the entrance where I was supposed to meet a potential client named Jonathan Spurrier. Over the phone he said he was referred to me by Danielle Cardoso, an heiress to one of the largest sugar plantations in Brazil. I've done a lot of work for Dani over the years. She lives right off of Connecticut Avenue along Embassy Row among the very wealthy and influential elite of Washington, D.C. She has referred many clients my way. Her connections with foreign diplomats, Senators and CEO's gives her ties to some of the most powerful, influential, egotistical and self-serving human beings which all happen to be dwelling in one central geographic location.

I glanced at my watch, then back across the street. He was late. Over the phone this guy was very hard to read. He was nervous and cagey, yet somehow seemed controlling and overly sure of himself. He intrigued me on one level, yet on another, made my little Spidey Sense start tingling.

I had time to kill. I picked up my laptop from the passenger seat, clicked on the browser and opened my e-mail. I clicked on a message from Lieutenant Grover with D.C. Metropolitan Homicide. He's a big guy, barrel chest, dark skinned and close cropped hair. I used to work for the man. He's a good detective. He relies too much on theory and inductive reasoning like profiling, but he's good. He runs the department with an iron fist and is willing to shield his people from the rain of bullshit that seems to fall from the clouds of bureaucracy above.

The e-mail from Grover was a cold case file that I requested. I figured now that I was retired I would do some volunteer work for the department and try to see if I could clean up some unsolved cases. Grover's men are very good but are usually loaded down with current cases, so he was happy to have me go back through cold cases for him.

D.C. is a busy city. A couple of million lawyers and politicians and lobbyists and CEO's all scurrying around each other like a bunch of ants at a political picnic, vying for any little bread crumbs of power they can scavenge. It attracts a lot of scandals, under the table deals and back alley exchanges. It also attracts a lot of crooks, the elected kind, the corporate kind and the deadly kind. D.C. used to be the murder capital of America. It's tamer now, but keeping it that way is a lot of work for the men and women in blue. I figured if I could help out then it was a way to give something back. If nothing else I owed that to Lieutenant Grover for all the headaches and ulcers I had given him.

As I glanced through the documents I reached over and grabbed a thermos from the passenger seat along with a ceramic mug I had pinched years ago from a diner. I poured a steaming black cup of joe and set the thermos aside. I leaned back and sipped it while I listened to the rain and reviewed the files.

Rain is a good companion. It calms and lulls the brain. It's got cadence and a constant rhythm, kinda like good bluesy jazz music. It's nice to have in the background while you're working.

At some point I glanced up and saw a man standing in the entryway of the brownstone buttoning a Burberry overcoat and staring out as if looking for someone. I shifted my Volkswagen into drive and pulled away from the curb, easing up to a position across from the archway. The man looked out. I lowered my window and waved. He stepped from the shadows, crossed the street and came around the car. In one motion he opened the passenger side door and dropped into the seat.

I stuck out my hand. "Frank Goulet."

The gentleman took my hand weakly and said, "Jonathan."

His wrinkled clothing and disheveled hair made him look lost and pathetic, like a wet kitten brought in from the rain. He didn't look like someone who was used to ever having a hair out of place. In his current state it was hard to tell if he was one of the egocentric elitists like most of Dani's friends, but who knows, the night was young.

I cast him a sideways glance. "Where to Jonathan Spurrier?"

"Do you know any place that's discreet where we can talk?"

"Sure, that's one thing about being an ex-cop, you know where all the good pubs are."

He didn't respond to my comment, so I just I took my foot off the brake and eased the car forward, paying attention to traffic and giving him some personal space.

As I negotiated the wet streets and

pedestrians who were darting out from between parked cars I glanced several times at my passenger. He was squeegeeing the water off his face with the palm of his delicate hand. He had long thin fingers and manicured nails. I handed him some napkins. He didn't say thank you, but simply took them dutifully as if I was his mother telling him to wipe his mouth after eating.

I glanced down at my own hands on the steering wheel. My fingers were like thick little sausages. The knuckles were callused and scarred from decades of hitting a heavy bag, breaking boards and occasionally someone's thick head.

I drove five blocks and pulled into a parking space on 24th Street across from Ian's Pub. We both made a mad dash for the door and were soaked by the time we made it inside.

Chapter 2

The pub was dimly lit and packed with people. The air inside was musty with the smell of wet clothes and hair. I spotted an empty table and pushed my way through, negotiating the crowd. As I was dropping my coat over the back of a chair, a pale, freckly-faced brunette appeared at my elbow. She looked to be about thirty and definitely gave a nice Irish feeling to the atmosphere.

"What can I get for you two?" She asked. I glanced at Spurrier.

"What kind of drinks do you serve in a place like this?" He replied. He was clearly a fish out of water.

I turned to her and said, "Just bring us two Guinnesses."

We sat down. As we settled in I took a moment to study him more closely. Jonathan Spurrier was middle-aged, good looking, clean cut, with pale skin and perfectly trimmed brown hair he wore in a David Bowie style. He was wearing a little eyeliner around his eyes. His frame was tall and lanky, with broad shoulders. He wore a black Armani Herringbone shirt which he kept buttoned all the way up and it was offset by a white belt. Despite the fact that he looked wet, wrinkled, tired and restless, I could tell by the way he looked around the room with disdain, as if he was better than those around him, that normally he was a person who was used to being in control and showing off his good looks and money.

"On the phone you said this was urgent," I stated.

Spurrier glanced left and right to see if anyone was listening. Then he stared down at the table to collect his thoughts.

"I have," he paused, "committed a small indiscretion, a peccadillo really, that may have some rather large repercussions."

"Hm, all of this angst over a small indiscretion."

He shifted in his chair and cleared his throat. "Well, I work for an agency which deals in sensitive, highly classified information."

"Are we talking government or private sector here?"

He stared at me with an air of incredulity. "Please, do I dress like a public servant? No Mr. Goulet, I own a brilliant company which deals in technologies with various nuclear and military applications."

"Go on."

Spurrier looked around nervously to see if anyone was watching us or overheard what he had said. Everyone in the pub was talking and laughing and didn't seem to give a rat's ass about me and the wet kitten. He looked back down at the table and was about to speak when the waitress set two glasses of Guinness on the table. I looked up.

"What's your name darlin'?"

"Dominique."

"I think my friend here needs to imbibe something a little stronger."

Spurrier looked at me. I narrowed my eyes as I studied him a moment, sizing him up. "Could you bring my friend a White Russian?"

"Certainly," Dominique replied.

Spurrier relaxed slightly. "Thanks, that was a good guess."

"More of a deduction really, it's an occupational habit." I reached over and dragged his glass to my side of the table. I wasn't going to waste a good Guinness.

We both sat quietly waiting. I was glad for the silence. This guy had a platinum coated chip on his shoulder that made listening to him like hearing fingernails on a blackboard.

Dominique arrived and slid the new drink in front of Spurrier. He looked at it. "A good drink for a cold, wet day."

"Amen," I said, raising my glass toward him.

When you have a client, or a date, with a lot of barriers between you, there is nothing like a few drinks to loosen them up. All the shrinks charge people a fortune to lay on a couch for six months just to get them to admit they have some Freudian yearning that is the root of all their woes. Yet they could have just taken them to a good pub and extracted far deeper admissions with a few good drinks.

I waited for Spurrier to have a few sips. I took a couple of quaffs out of my own glass. The Guinness was cold and thick and foamy on top. As his face eased up a little I said, "Alright, look, I get the gist. You are a contractor who deals in classified info and something's been compromised. Just tell me the details."

Spurrier took a long sip and set the glass on the table. He stared down at the glass, focusing on it like he was gazing into a crystal ball.

"I am the owner and CEO of a company called SPURRIER and FREEN Advanced Aerospace Ceramics. We deal mostly in ceramic materials for ultra-high temperature applications related to aerospace and nuclear energy technology. We hold several patents in the field and currently we have some of the hottest research going on related to thermal barrier coatings and experimental alloys." He paused to take a sip of his drink. He glanced around. No one in the pub seemed to give a damn about our conversation.

"The particular thermal barrier coatings we are working on have direct applications for the military, for use in things like Tomahawk missiles. You see, turbofan engines are exposed to high heat and stress. Special metal alloys and thermal barrier coatings are always being researched to reduce the impact from the heat and stress. About two years ago we had a major breakthrough in creating a new type of ceramic topcoat out of a rare earth zirconate. We are on the verge of producing it, which could win us huge contracts with the big companies that produce the turbofan engines for both military and commercial applications."

"Congratulations," I said.

"Yeah," Jonathan said, the side of his mouth twisting up into a slight ironic smile.

"That's all very interesting, but it's just twaddle at this point. Tell me why I'm here."

He lowered his voice. "Her name is Charlotte. We went out last night. I uh, hired her to escort me to a private party. Afterward, we, well, I think you get the picture."

"She's a hooker."

"Well, she's an escort."

"Apples and oranges Jonathan, she's a hooker."

"Could you keep your voice down?" He whispered, looking around to see if anyone was paying attention.

"Go on, continue, so what happened?"

"She must have slipped something into my drink. I woke up the next morning and my wallet and briefcase were gone."

"So what was in the briefcase?"

"My briefcase has classified documents not only about our research, formulas and specs, but also about military research regarding specs of their engines currently in use in cruise missiles, and target and reconnaissance drones. I had files with notes from our trips to the U.S. Army Research Laboratory at the Aberdeen Proving Grounds."

I took a swig of my Guinness and stared at Jonathan, studying him a long moment as I held it in my mouth and then let it slide down my throat. "Hm, so you took highly classified information to your little soiree with the hooker," I stated, letting the words hang in the air between us.

I took another long sip of Guinness. I pointed at his hands with my chin and said, "Your scuffed up knuckles and flecks of red under the skin, suggests you played kinda rough last night with Charlotte."

He smiled and rubbed his knuckles with his left hand. "I pay Charlotte well to do certain things."

"Sounds like you've seen her before."

"Many times."

I took another long sip. "You into the rough stuff Jonathan, a little S&M? You get off by inflicting pain and roughing up women?"

"It's all in good fun."

"Maybe for you. How rough do you play with these hookers?"

"That's not really germane to what we are discussing here."

"Not germane? Well, maybe this hooker was tired of you beating on her and decided to go for the big paycheck and just took your wallet and briefcase and bolted."

"No, Charlotte likes it. I pay her well. We have a good time."

I was starting to get pissed. I've dealt with dozens of people just like Jonathan over the years who get turned on brutalizing people. They're like teenagers who get off beating up winos in alleys or gang bangers that like to beat random people to within an inch of their life. They like it. I pushed on. "Where did you go to do it with this escort?"

"We met at a hotel called The Modicum Hotel."

"I thought you said she escorted you to a private party?"

"Oh, well, I uh, I met her at the hotel. That was the private party."

"See this is good Jonathan. You're starting to really open up and bear your soul to me here."

"Look, this isn't easy to tell someone."

"Go on, tell me about the briefcase. If you were meeting an escort why in the hell did you have your briefcase with you?"

"It was after work. I was taking it home and didn't want to leave it in my car. I thought I would just be in the hotel with her for an hour or two."

"And have you used The Modicum, before?"

"Yes."

"How many times?"

"Many."

"Are we talking a dozen times, four dozen times, how many?"

"Your questions are inane detective. How is it relevant how many times I have used this place?"

I spoke to him slowly, as if I was speaking to a first grader. "Basic mugging 101, if, somebody wants to rob you, they scope out your habits Jonathan. And if, they know where you go, and you have a pattern, it makes it pretty damn easy. So, to get back to my inane little line of questioning, how often do you use this place?"

Jonathan didn't like being put in his place. He looked around and spoke softly. "About once a week."

"Do you stay there for other reasons besides hooking up with escorts?"

"No, I use other hotels for business."

"So, you hire hookers once a week?"

"Sometimes more, I have a large sexual appetite."

"That's not how I would have put it, but moving right along, how did you find this escort service?"

"A Senator I have close connections to recommended them."

"You seem like a smart guy Jonathan."

"I went to MIT."

"Congratulations. But you aren't real bright about how you safeguard your classified information."

"Like I said, a small indiscretion on my part."

"No, an act of stupidity on your part."

The corners of his mouth lifted slightly into a sardonic, arrogant smile. "Like you said before detective, apples and oranges."

God he was an arrogant prick. Dani was going to owe me big time for this one. I pushed on with my questioning. "So do you always arrange these little soirees directly with her or with her agency?"

"Her agency, actually. It's through a

particular man named Dexter Deahl."

"Alright, so, tell me about her," I said.

His eyes lit up as he started to describe her. "She's gorgeous. A blonde with long hair and huge blue eyes. She's young and innocent looking, and very athletic."

"How young are we talking?"

"Oh, I don't know, 17, maybe 18. I don't know. I don't really care."

I paused. My beer glass was sitting on the table. My fingers were absentmindedly turning it around and around on its napkin as I stared at Jonathan.

"Look, I'm not hiring you to be my confessor or my priest. If I like to hire women to fulfill my fantasies, that's my business. And you know what? I pay her damn well for it."

"That's what you fantasize about, roughing up women?"

"Look Goulet, we're all big boys here. So let's talk cold turkey. I know my eccentricities are not legal. That's why I am not going to the police. I need someone like you, a private investigator who can keep this little indiscretion confidential."

I stared down at my glass as I continued twirling it around. I was trying to control myself. "You know Jonathan, what you need is a shrink, not a private investigator."

He sat staring at me with an arrogant condescending smile. I could see in his eyes that his self-righteousness was like a Teflon armor that just caused my comments to roll right off.

"Mr. Goulet, can we get back to the problem at hand, my briefcase?"

"No, I think we're done here. I'll get the check."

I started looking around the room for Dominique.

"Oh, get off you high horse Goulet. I deal with powerful people and have the money to get whatever the hell I want. And if I want to beat the hell of some little whor…………"

My hand reacted before I could stop it. I was across the table and my open palm caught him square on the side of the head, knocking him out of his chair. I stood above him.

"Did you like that Jonathan? How does it feel to get hit? You think the women like that?"

His face turned beet red as he scrambled to his feet. He was huffing and puffing and his eyes darted around the room at the faces staring at us. His cheek was bright crimson where my hand had connected with him. His little David Bowie style haircut was disheveled, and part of it was sticking straight up in the air so he looked like a school boy with a cowlick. His fists were doubled up by his sides like he was ready to fight. I glared at him from across the table. Both of our drinks had spilled and the glasses were laying on the floor.

Everyone in the pub was staring at us. Dominique was hurrying across the room and a very large man with a barrel chest was right behind her.

I continued to look hard at Jonathan, staring him down. There was gravel in my voice as I spoke, from years of experience being in fights with guys who would have shot or stabbed Jonathan just for looking at them the wrong way. "You wanna take a swing at me you goddamn little perv? Take your best shot." I really hoped he'd take a swing.

Suddenly he looked hesitant. Dominique and the bouncer arrived. I turned to her and said, "I'm sorry. He just told me he slept with my wife and I lost control for a second." Everyone turned their eyes on Jonathan and began to murmur things about him that were unintelligible.

"Here," I said, pulling out my wallet to pay for the drinks. I handed her two twenty dollar bills. "That's for your trouble."

"That's alright," she replied. "I don't blame you for smacking him." She turned and glared at Jonathan who was looking more and more uncomfortable as he looked around the room at the people staring at him.

"Get your coat," I stated to Jonathan.

He did as he was told. I apologized to Dominique once again and pushed my way through the crowd toward the door. People parted like the Red Sea as we walked through, scooting their chairs out of the way and staring up hard at Jonathan as we passed by. All I could think to myself at that moment was how much harder they would be staring if they knew the real reason I smacked him.

When we got outside we stood under the awning covering the walkway by the entrance. The rain was coming down hard. Jonathan pulled on his overcoat and without saying a word he stepped out into the rain and began walking up the street. I watched him as the details of his outline began to blur into the darkness and the streaks of the falling rain. I stood for a moment staring out at the rain feeling annoyed and pissed. God I could use a good Scotch. I turned my collar up, stuck my hands down into my pockets and walked in the other direction. I knew another pub two blocks up where they always kept good bottles of twelve year old Glenmorangie for the people who were serious about their Scotch.

Chapter 3

The next morning I was up at 6:00. I've never been one to sleep in. The rain was still falling, but it was lighter, making dull tapping sounds on the window pane. My apartment is a studio, second floor, in an old brick Victorian, above a bar called Fiona's. Fiona was happy to lease it to me since I am a retired cop and can keep an eye on the place when it's closed, so she gives me a reduced rate on the rent. It's right on M Street in Georgetown, which is usually packed with bustling Washingtonians, tourists, shoppers and graduate students. The busyness of it keeps me company.

Fiona starts serving lunch at 11:00 a.m. They do some good Buffalo wings, a really wicked chili and shepherd's pie, have fifteen beers on tap and make the best Reuben in D.C. Every morning the smell of fresh coffee, bacon and meats cooking usually stirs me from my lethargy and procrastination.

Georgetown is one of several hip pockets of D.C. along with Adams Morgan and Dupont Circle which are all about as hip as Washington, D.C. gets. There are art galleries, bars, eateries, cafés and a million shops all installed for the benefit of the wealthy people who live there and the more upscale tourists that want to come to the nation's capital. The C&O Canal Towpath, Rock Creek Parkway and the Potomac River all border Georgetown. It still has lots of trees, steep streets and buildings from the early 1900's. It makes you feel like you have stepped into an Edward Hopper painting.

I sat looking out my window onto M Street with a fresh cup of jet black coffee while checking e-mails to see if any new information had come in on several cases that were ongoing. One was a typical extramarital affair. My client was a wealthy professional woman who had married a Jody, a deadbeat guy who looks for rich women to support them. In this case my client married a man ten years her junior with a nice set of equipment she thought would keep her bed warm at night. The problem is he was keeping a lot of other beds warm as well. I try to stay away from too many of these cases but I like expensive wine and good food, so there you go.

My other case was the theft of a small Picasso sketch from a private residence in Dupont Circle. The picture had been swiped by a live-in maid who skipped town and vanished off the face of the earth.

As I checked my e-mails the street below was filled with people in business suits and dresses carrying umbrellas and moving like a bunch or bumper cars as their umbrellas bumped and veered around each other. As I sipped my coffee and stared out at the worker ants below I felt as snug as a bug in a rug.

By 10:30 I had showered and shaved and headed downstairs to meet Dani for an early lunch. We usually meet at least once a week at Fiona's to touch base and catch up. Fiona's bar doubles as my office. It's convenient and if business is slow I can always get an early start on acquiring a nice agreeable level of alcohol in my bloodstream.

Fiona looked as fresh as ever as I popped out of the upstairs doorway to the pub. She is 48 years old, has a youthful face with a smattering of freckles and the hard eyes of a person who is street savvy with a contrasting warm smile. She's a beautiful woman. Her big head of curly red hair is always pulled back in a ponytail while she's working. She has tattoos on her neck, right shoulder and in some places that rarely see the sunshine. There is something genuine and fresh about Fiona.

"Mornin' Frank," she called out.

"Hey lady, how you doin' this morning?"

"You got a second?"

"I have two seconds for you."

"Alright, I'll bring you some coffee in a minute and fill you in."

I shuffled across the floor to my regular booth and set my laptop down. There are two sets of booths in Fiona's. One set runs along the ten foot tall plate glass windows that look out onto M street. The other set of booths are along the 100 year old dark chestnut walls that run toward the back of the building. I always sit at the last booth along the windows like a cat sitting in the sunshine trying to soak up the solar warmth.

Fiona's bar has twelve foot high ceilings and tends to be a bit dark inside. The long wooden bar and raised panel walls are dark chestnut from another era. It's gorgeous and inviting. A good atmosphere for a bar, but tends to be a little cold inside if you're sitting all day.

I slid into the booth and fired up my laptop as Fiona stepped up to the table.

"What's up?" I asked.

"I have two guys who seem like they're casing the place. They've come in the last two nights, sit quietly nursing a few light beers and seemed to be scoping everything out. They're still here at closing and then stand across the street as Tom closes everything down."

I glanced out the window. "You mean like right over there by the bank?"

"Yeah."

"You got a description for me?"

"Mutt and Jeff, one huge football player type and one thin lanky junkie type with oily hair. They both look like they're in their mid to late twenties."

"I'll try to come down the next few nights and keep an eye out for them."

"Thanks." She smiled and looked relieved. "So Frank, you want chili or a Rueben for lunch?"

"I am pretty predictable aren't I?"

"Hey, it makes it easy on me?"

"What did I have yesterday?"

"Chili."

"Well then, just to be different, let's go with a Rueben."

She smiled, shook her head and turned and went back in the kitchen. I turned my attention to the computer screen. A quick search of the Washington Metropolitan Police page updated me on the most recent incident reports filed in the News Room section of the webpage. There was one Death Investigation on 17th Street, a couple of Burglaries, shots fired in Southeast and a Homicide on Alabama Avenue.

I was finishing my daily updates as a steaming hot plate with a Reuben on it was slipped onto the table beside me. I looked up at

Fiona and smiled. "Thank you darlin'."

She pinched my cheek hard and smiled. It hurt. I couldn't let her see that so I just kept smiling.

As Fiona headed back to the kitchen I flipped the top piece of rye over to assemble my sandwich, picked it up and sunk my teeth into it. A good Reuben is the crowning glory of what Corned Beef is all about. I could care less about the age old argument of whether the Reuben was first invented in Omaha late one night at a hotel for some guy's playing poker or whether it was invented by the owner of a New York deli. What matters is that it is made right. At Fiona's they use good tangy sauerkraut that's got depth to it. They use fresh Russian dressing, instead of Thousand Island. Their corned beef is made in-house and moist and the sandwich doesn't leak dressing or kraut when you sink your teeth into it. Add a cold Beck's to wash it down and you have a little slice of heaven on rye.

Dani was late, but I was enjoying the Reuben so much that I didn't mind. Every bite filled my mouth with sweet and tangy sensations. I looked around the bar and noticed a bunch of the regulars starting to filter in.

One guy named Mitch is there most mornings. He orders a Jack and Coke first thing when he comes in the door. I've seen him in there still looking steady as a rock and tossing them back at 10:00 at night. He's like a well-trained Olympic marathon runner, knowing how to pace himself for the long haul. He's a ruggedly handsome guy, always has a good one liner for comebacks and an easy going smile. Every night he goes home with some attractive lady. It hasn't gone unnoticed by me that he always hits on the ladies who seem to have a lot of money and frequently are married. I don't know what the hell he does for a living, but it seems the ladies shower him with fine clothes and a place to spend the night. To me he seems like a Jody, but hey, if the women who take care of him are happy and don't mind spending the dough, who am I to judge? I suppose you could argue it's a form of prostitution with him being his own pimp and simply cutting out the middle man, or woman. I guess we all have our innate skills we put to work in one way or another.

Greta seems to come and go at Fiona's. She's elegant, classy, seems to be loaded with cash and is usually three sheets to the wind by early afternoon. She's always decked out in dark clothing and lots of jewelry. Clearly over forty, thin, with a pointy nose and a pinched face, Greta hangs on the edge of conversations tossing back Martinis until they finally catch up to her. She's nice enough but seems lonely.

Then there's Lenny, your classic little internet rich geek. He's there many mornings firing up his laptop, putting lots of hot sauce on anything he grabs from the buffet. He alternates all day between double espressos and Redbull and vodkas. He's affable and speaks loudly. Not a bad kid, it's just a little obnoxious to see a frat boy type who hit easy street straight out of college. He floats in and out throughout the day and apparently lives nearby.

Perhaps the one I adore the most is Mara. She is an investor and part owner of Fiona's. She's an elegant black woman, with large expressive eyes and long lashes. She has a thin wispy frame but strong arms. Her neck is always adorned with pearls or some elegant jewelry which is never ostentatious and she is always in a dress which shows off her figure but is never too revealing. Everything about her shows a certain class which stands out. I think if Audrey Hepburn was ever reincarnated as anything other than an actress she would have been Mara. Mara always sits at the bar and talks to Fiona. Mitch hits on her incessantly and she seems amused and tolerant, like someone who tolerates a small spoiled child who is always expecting to be given a cookie. What I like most about Mara, is that instead of being a martini kind of lady, which can sometimes be a snooty cry for, "look at me, I'm classy,"she enjoys a nice 12 year old Scotch. And she sips it with relish.

Fiona came back with an espresso for me as Dani walked in the door. Every head in the joint, men and women alike, turned to stare. She has that effect on people. When she walks across a room you can imagine her on a runway for some big fashion magazine. She has long straight dark hair that swings across her back in perfect rhythm with her hips. Her legs are toned like an athlete and her backside is something men's eyes are hypnotized by like a hypnotist swinging a watch back and forth before them. She always dresses in skirts and high heels, showing off those ten million dollar legs. And if all of that weren't enough, her olive skin, large green eyes and puffy lips along with firm shapely breasts makes for something that men can and do fantasize about routinely. But the best part about Dani is that she rarely ever notices the effect she is having on all those poor bastards.

I watched Dani advance across the room as I said thank you to Fiona.

"You are a vision as always," I said.

She didn't smile. As she got close to the table she said, "Damn Frank, is it just that hot-headed French temperament of yours or what? Jonathan told me you slapped him."

"I did."

She sat down across from me. The sun coming in through the window made the green of her eyes the color of the surf at the shore. "Frank, I'm sending some high dollar clients your way. You don't treat them like drug dealers in a back alley."

"You look more beautiful than ever," I

said with a smile.

"I am serious Frank."

"So am I."

My charm wasn't working. I guess it only worked on people I had handcuffed who were sitting in the back of a patrol car. Fiona came up to the table and started to ask Dani if she wanted anything. Dani just turned those big Brazilian eyes on her, which had changed from their usual exotic alluring beauty to a raging sea, and Fiona said, "I'll come back."

"Seriously Frank, Jonathan is no one to trifle with."

"Did he tell you why I slapped him?"

"He said you found out that he had an affair and you were just a prude."

"He gets off beating the hell out of young hookers. This particular one is probably underage to boot. He's white trash dressed in Armani. Someone needed to slap his ass a long time ago."

Dani looked shocked. "God, he really is a pervert."

"Exactly, except my sentiments were a little stronger than that."

"So you really slapped him?"

"I just reacted on a visceral level. I didn't think about it. You know how sometimes you see something that is so nauseating it makes you puke? Well, he was sitting there with that nasty, pompous, self-righteous look on his face telling me about that shit and I just reacted."

"I probably would have hit him too, but look Frank, as disgusting as he is I really need you to help him."

I looked away from Dani while I put a heaping spoonful of sugar into my espresso. I was giving myself a moment to decide whether my allegiance to Dani or my natural aversion to pompous rich elitists like Jonathan would win out. I stirred the coffee. I could feel Dani watching me. I lifted the small ceramic cup to my lips and took a loud sip. It was strong and bitter and sweet mixed together. I set it down and looked at her.

"Dani, just being around him makes me feel like taking a bath in Purell."

"I know, but his company could go under."

"It couldn't happen to a nicer guy. By the way, Fiona makes a damn good espresso, you want one?" I took another long sip.

"God Frank, you French people, all you think about is food."

"First off, I'm an American. My parents are French. Secondly, that's not true, we simply know how to step back and appreciate life. There's always some tragedy in the world, some whack job killing people, some government about to push the button. You need to learn to step back and take a break Dani, turn off that crap and enjoy your food, your coffee, your friends."

"Frank sometimes I just feel like reaching across the table and smacking you."

"If you did I would have to shoot you."

She just shook her head back and forth. "Frank, I really need your help here. I am the largest shareholder in his company. I started investing in him several years ago before they started getting the big patents and contracts. They are brilliant. Their research and development has so many applications and they deal with most of the biggest ceramic tech companies. The particular research they are pioneering could help push turbofan engines into a much higher performance level, and bring in a lot of money. Their shares are already edging up."

"He's morally debauched. I don't want anything to do with him." I held my espresso cup up to her and said, "the only ceramics I wish to deal with are the ones that hold a good cup of coffee."

Dani shook her head back and forth in annoyance. "Look Frank, you know I don't condone his behavior, but I need you to help him."

I took another sip of coffee and looked into her beautiful eyes. "Did you know that he wears eye liner?"

"A lot of men do that nowadays. He's a metrosexual."

"Metrosexual? Isn't it wonderful how we love to soften all the labels for weirdoes by branding them with innocuous terms so they don't' get their feelings hurt?"

"Hey, it's getting to be more hip. Some men wear other make up as well."

I responded with a slight grunt as I thought about that. What ever happened to men just slapping on a little Old Spice after shaving? Dani sat waiting.

"You really want me to help this guy?" I asked.

"Look Frank, he might be depraved and morally debauched, but let me lay this out in simple terms. I stand to lose a lot of money if it gets out that his plans were stolen and someone else gets the technology. You know how volatile the market is. Their shares could plummet."

I sipped my coffee and stared out the window. Dani had helped me a lot over the years. I owed her a lot.

I shook my head back and forth and let out a sigh. "It's a good thing you're so gorgeous and charming."

Dani looked relieved. "Alright, I'll call Jonathan and let him know."

"Look Dani, don't get your hopes up. On the one hand it's entirely possible this hooker who stole his briefcase had no idea what was in it and thought she would just go through it to take whatever she could get. It's also possible that this is some high level corporate spying, or worse, a foreign government and they hired this hooker to do their dirty work. She may now be floating in the Potomac or Anacostia River as we speak. This may need to be something for the feds to handle."

"You think this could be that big?"

"This is D.C., the spy capital of the world. He deals in technology with military and nuclear applications."

"Hm, well, whatever the case, you're the best Frank. You'll get to the bottom of it. Maybe your girlfriend, the D.A. can help. She usually helps you right?"

"She's not really my girlfriend, and she's an Assistant D.A."

"Whatever she is, anyway she can help. Listen, I spoke with Jonathan this morning. He wants to meet you for lunch. Talk to him and some of his people and see where it goes. You also might want to go speak with his wife Lily."

"Does she know about all the seedy stuff he's into?"

"Oh yeah, she is a brilliant woman who accepts his eccentricities."

"Don't gloss over his actions by calling them eccentricities."

"How about quirks?"

"They're not quirks, or foibles or little idiosyncrasies. He's a wealthy, spoiled pervert, who is used to getting whatever he wants?"

"Talk to his wife and to his employees and see what you think."

"Well, you are going to owe me big time for this one my friend."

"I'll tell you what, I'll pay for a long trip to Paris for you. You can stay in my apartment there for as long as you want."

I shook my head back and forth. "You need to throw in a case of a good Bordeaux from 1990, like maybe some bottles of a Margaux, Latour or Pétrus."

"You are terrible Frank. I'll tell you what, I have about six bottles left of some Haut-Brion from 1990."

"Deal."

Chapter 4

A luncheon was set for me to meet with Jonathan and his partner Ted Freen. I suggested we meet at a place that wasn't one of their usual haunts since there was a chance of corporate spying. I wanted some place that was neutral and discreet.

Since it was my call where we would eat and it was on their tab, I decided I might as well get a high dollar meal out of it. I chose a pricey Italian restaurant in Northeast that makes their own pasta and bread in house and also has an exceptional wine list.

We met outside the restaurant at 1:00. The rain had stopped completely now. The sun was beginning to poke holes through the cloud cover and the humidity was starting to rise. It was still chilly outside, typical for March weather in DC.

As Jonathan approached the restaurant with his partner they made for an interesting contrast. Jonathan in his hip regalia, was wearing a pink Armani shirt with a thin black tie and his white belt. His partner, who looked to be about the same age, wore a three piece Valentino suit, dark blue, a more classy and traditional style, offset with a yellow silk tie. His hair was closely cropped and neat, very military looking. In fact everything about his physique, his slightly swaggering gait and athletic body suggested a military background.

Jonathan was smiling as they approached, as if nothing bad had ever happened between us. He was arrogant and had a kind of cocksure attitude about him that was annoying. I put on my best face and offered my hand to him as they approached.

"Frank, I knew you would come around," Spurrier said, looking pleased with himself.

"You have Dani to thank for that," I noted.

"Well, this is Ted Freen. Ted and I met when we were in graduate school. He's a Stanford man. We started this company together."

"It's nice to meet you Ted," I said.

Ted looked me directly in the eyes and had a very manly handshake that was strong but not competitive like he needed to prove something. We headed inside and were seated.

The waiter handed us our menus and took our drink order. Jonathan ordered a Mojito. Ted ordered a martini, Grey Goose, straight up with two olives. It surprised me.

"You don't look like a martini kinda guy," I noted.

Ted looked at me like I was speaking in Croatian.

"I'm sorry, what?"

"You don't strike me as a martini man."

"Really, well what would you think I drink?"

"You seem more like a Tom Collins kinda guy."

"Huh, I did used to drink Tom Collins all the time," he confessed.

"Thought so," I noted. "And how long have you been sailing? I would guess quite some time."

Ted furrowed his eyebrows. "How in the world do you know that?"

"Your hands have the type of callouses that come from years of ropes sliding across them. Your tan looks natural. Your cheeks are burnished from the wind and the back of your neck is red and deeply wrinkled from years of being in the sun. It's the kind of deep burn that farmers, construction workers, fisherman and sailors share."

"Well, that is quite a trick detective," Ted said.

"It's not a trick, just simple deductive reasoning."

"He's quite the detective," Jonathan stated dryly.

I sat back and let the two of them chat. Ted was a traditional guy, and obviously very intelligent, but seemed like someone who dressed and drank by how he thought he should do it. The two men seemed like polar opposites. I looked at the wine list and ordered a nice red Cannonau wine.

They chatted between themselves about some work matters while we waited for drinks. I was glad. It gave me a chance to watch how the two of them interacted. I had the sense that Jonathan was speaking a little louder than necessary at times, as if he wanted me to hear how much he knew about things and that he was in charge. He used a lot of scientific lingo that went right over my head. Ted on the other hand spoke in a quieter, deeper voice. He listened well and responded primarily. It all suggested that Jonathan was the dominant partner. But in truth, at a gut level, I sensed that Ted actually understood what they were talking about on a deeper intellectual level. He discreetly corrected Jonathan twice regarding figures he was quoting, but each time he did it he suggested the numbers, gracefully letting

Jonathan save face. It was a fascinating interaction.

When our drinks arrived we all ordered our food. I ordered a chilled soup made with yellow tomatoes, crab and fava beans, to be followed by a risotto with black truffles and lamb. The way I figured it, even if the meeting went south at least I would get a great meal out of it.

"So, Mr. Goulet, where do we begin looking in a case like this? I imagine you've handled things like this before. " Ted asked.

"Call me Frank. First off, it's dangerous to begin hypothesizing before you have real data. Some detectives like to use inductive reasoning and will tell you statistically that cases like this are typically committed by such and such types of people. That is very misleading detective work. You never start by looking at similar cases. It may help later, once you have some facts, but in the beginning it taints your perspective. We take things one step at a time and look for facts."

"Okay," Ted replied.

I continued. "First, it is possible this woman was hired to steal Jonathan's briefcase and the company's secrets. But it's also possible that she was simply ripping off one of her clients like some hookers do. Since we don't know the motive let's start by finding out more about who knows your business, who might be interested, if any companies have approached you about buying you out. Do you have competitors who might resort to corporate theft?"

"Good god, that list could stretch from here to China," Jonathan said.

"Exactly, or Russia or North Korea," I countered.

"Yes, there is that," Jonathan replied.

"Have you had any foreign governments approach you with offers, or at least expressing interest?"

"Of course, this is Washington. They all know who has the things they want."

"Any actual offers?"

"Yes, from the Russians, Chinese, India, Pakistan, Israel, North Korea……"

"I get the point. Have you ever had anyone try to break in or try to steal secrets from you before?"

"Of course," Jonathan's tone was condescending. It wasn't hard to imagine him as a little rich snot nosed brat throwing temper tantrums and demanding his mother to give him Captain Crunch instead of the nicely prepared eggs, bacon and toast she had labored over to prepare.

"You must have been a fractious child," I stated.

Jonathan looked at me and shook his head in annoyance. He pulled out his phone to check his messages. I have to give it to him, he didn't get ruffled easily. He was smooth.

"What room did you stay in at The Modicum?"

"Room 511."

"I'll check it out."

The conversation went on for an hour and a half as we ate. The food was good and I was a good boy and restrained myself from smacking Jonathan again, although it wasn't easy. I got a list of all of their employees and they promised to give me access to all background information on them. I also got a description of what was in the briefcase, files, computer discs, etc. I told Jonathan to get in touch with his credit card companies and ask them if any purchases had been made on his stolen cards.

I finished off my bottle of Cannonau and decided I better switch to coffee at that point. Jonathan went through four mojitos. Ted kept it at two martinis and only added things to the conversation when Jonathan wasn't dominating it. I told them I would need to bring an associate in on this, who is former military and also a retired DC cop, so he had high clearances on two levels. They didn't bat an eye at this or even ask what the price tag for all of my time was going to be. That's one of those little things that is always fascinating about clients with extreme wealth, they don't really care what things cost. It must be nice.

Chapter 5

It was a little after 6:00 in the evening when Angel showed up at my apartment. I opened the door to see his enormous body, scarred face and shaved head grinning at me with that crazy ass stare of his. He threw his arms open wide, "Frankieeeee, what's up?"

"Hey Angel, get your ass in here."

He stepped in and wrapped his giant arms around me. I am five 5' 10" and tip the scales at 205, with little body fat. Angel makes me look tiny.

He picked me up off the ground and finished his big ass burly hug. I have worked with a lot of men in my life who are tough as nails and crazier than hell, but Angel is literally the craziest bastard I have ever known, present company excepted. The man is fearless and has probably been in more bar fights, consumed more Jack and Coke and shot more people in the line of duty than any twenty cops or ten soldiers put together. He was a U.S. Army sniper before he came onto DC Metro and became their top shooter on the SWAT team. His number of kills in Iraq, Afghanistan and in other nations where the U.S. wasn't technically supposed to be is a staggering figure. His moniker Angel was given to him for saving the lives of a platoon in Iraq that walked into an ambush. His rifle and scope watched over that little band of soldiers and kept them as safe as the fiery sword of Saint Michael the Archangel. His nickname followed him onto the police force as well. He had pulled the trigger on numerous suspects in hostage situations and was never calmer than when he had the safety off and someone in his sights.

He set me down and walked on in to my apartment. "You wanna beer?" He asked over his shoulder as he headed for my refrigerator.

"I'm already three ahead of you brother."

"That means you're already four behind me," he called back.

"What the hell have you been doing today?"

"I was out at the range and then had lunch with The Boys Club."

"I should have figured. How are the boys?"

"Ornery," he shot back. I heard the fridge door open and the sound of bottles clacking together as he pulled a couple from the fridge.

"Was Burrito Man there?" I asked.

"No, he's out of town giving a seminar." Angel sauntered back into the room. He had removed his big black leather jacket and was only wearing a black sleeveless shirt now. His enormous arms were covered from wrists to armpits with a collection of tattoos that had various images of skulls, snakes, daggers, guns and other things associated with killing things. When he was going sleeveless and you saw the tattoos and the long scar that laid horizontal across his right cheek which was a shrapnel scar from a mortar round, he could look a little intimidating. The earring he wore in his right ear was a live .40 caliber round and it added a nice touch to his appearance.

He handed me a beer and was smiling as he sat down.

"What the hell are you so happy about?" I asked, taking the already open beer and tilting it up to my lips.

"I'm excited to see you brother," he said as he leaned back, extending his giant left arm up onto the back of the couch and taking a long pull on his beer. He finished his sip and then extended the bottle out before him to examine it. "What the hell kind of beer is this?"

"You didn't even notice? You just down

anything that is in a beer bottle without looking at what it is?"

"Dos Equis?" He asked, looking quizzically as he studied the bottle.

"The beer of The Most Interesting Man in the World. Haven't you seen the commercials?"

"What is that, you think that's you now? The Dos Equis man?"

"I am pretty interesting, but nobody is as interesting as the Dos Equis man."

"Hm," he grunted, tilting the bottle back up and taking another swig. He swallowed and then looked at the bottle again. "Huh, it's good."

"Of course it's good. You don't think The Most Interesting Man in the World would drink it if it wasn't good."

He shook his head back and forth, tilting the beer up one more time and sucked the whole thing down. He got up from the couch and headed back to the kitchen. "You want another one?" He hollered over his shoulder. When he came back he took a seat and wanted to hear where we were with things.

Angel and I had worked together a long time. We retired at the same time two years ago. He made money on the side helping me with cases and tuning up sniper rifles for various agencies. His background made him in high demand for giving seminars and for coaching other SWAT teams around the nation. There wasn't a major police force he hadn't worked with on some level and consequently he probably never will have to worry about ever getting a DUI in any jurisdiction he travels in. He is loyal and faithful and has one hell of a sense of humor. There is no one I trust so completely.

"So you really slapped that little shit?"

"I did," I confessed.

"And he still hired you?" Angel had a quizzical look on his face, like he was having a hard time comprehending this.

"He did."

"And he wears eye liner?"

"He does."

Angel took another pull on his beer. "Huh, is he gay?"

"Maybe bi."

"Shit. And he likes beating up hookers?"

"Uh-huh." I took another pull on my beer.

"And he's richer than hell and good looking. Where the hell is the justice in this world?"

"That's why we're here," I replied.

"Huh, well, this will be interesting. Maybe when we're done and have the check in hand we can tie him up, pull his pants down and spank him a little, you know, like with a baseball bat. See how he likes it."

"I like the way you think. Hey, have you checked with your boss to see if you can get deep into this?" I asked.

"Yeah, Amy is good with it. But then you probably already knew that didn't you?"

"Hey, I know who wears the pants in your house. I always check with Amy before I talk to you."

He laughed. "You got that right brother. She's the boss. By the way, how's your lady doing?"

"I don't have a lady."

"You and Isa have been sleeping together for what like two years?"

"We're not dating. Now, let's get back to what we were talking about."

Angel looked at me with annoyance. I ignored him, reached over to the coffee table and picked up an envelope and handed it to him.

"What's this?" He asked.

"Name of the escort service, phone number, name of the guy Spurrier always talks to, info on the hotel, etc."

"How you want to handle this?"

"First off I need you to get down to The Modicum Hotel, ask when their dumpster is emptied. If it hasn't been emptied yet, then I need you to……

"Yeah, yeah, I got it boss, do some dumpster diving, fuuuuck," he said, tilting his beer up and taking a long pull on it.

"Hey, man, you know how it works. If this was a simple pinch then the odds are they ditched the briefcase and wallet within a few blocks."

"Got it chief. I'll check all the alleys and likely spots within four or five blocks."

"Alright, while you're doing that I called The Modicum and room 511 was available so I reserved it. I'm going down there shortly to look around. They said the maids have already cleaned it since night before last, but they said no one else has rented it, so it's worth a look." I paused to organize my thoughts. "Oh, have you been in touch with Dogbone?"

"Yeah, he and I are doing some contract stuff for the Agency."

"Good, well bring him in on this. Tell him we have a high paying client so expense is no issue. I need traces on phones from The Modicum, on Jonathan Spurrier, on SPURRIER AND FREEN and on a Chinese guy named Reggie. I'm sure that without calling in big favors from his cloak and dagger buddies he may not be able to fully tap the lines, but if he can't then at least trace them so we can see who they're talking to. All of their phone numbers are written here," I said as I handed Angel a paper with everyone's names on it. He studied it a moment, then looked up at me with a puzzled look.

"You want surveillance on Spurrier?"

"You know me, everyone is a suspect until I can cross them off the list."

"Alright, bug Spurrier, check."

"Alright, after searching the room I am going to start casing out the escort service, then the employees with the company, check out Spurrier's wife and some associates. Gotta get deep into Spurrier's contacts and find out who's been nosing around a little too much."

"Well, that's what your good at Sherlock."

We touched the necks of our beer bottles together as a little toast and chugged them down.

Chapter 6

It was 8:47 when I picked up my key at the front desk and rode the elevator up to room 511. The hotel was well maintained, with a nice tightly woven carpet in the hallways that had a classy pattern printed on it.

I got off the elevator on the fifth floor and went down to room 511. When I opened the door it had that musty smell of a room that has been closed up all day, the only air coming into it being from the heating unit attached under the window. The linens on the bed had that slightly burnt smell of polyester fiber that has been run through a drier on the highest setting, cooking and sterilizing the covers.

I closed the door behind me and stood looking around the room. Everything was firehouse clean. The carpet still had tracks in it from the vacuum cleaner. The bed sheets and covers were stretched tight and the pillows were perfectly fluffed. There were two big queen sized beds. Immediately images flashed through my mind of Jonathan being on one of those beds with the blonde-haired and blue-eyed Charlotte.

I took a deep breath and let it out to clear my mind as I gazed around the room. First looks are always the freshest, the least biased. There was nothing out of place. To my right was the bathroom door. I reached in and turned on the light. The whole room was one solid color of off white and as sterile looking as an operating room. I squatted down and visually scanned the floor. I stepped in, squatted again, looked around the base of the toilet. Nothing was out of place. I reached into the trashcan pulled the plastic bag back that was lining it. Sometimes the liner comes free and things fall down behind it, but, nothing this time.

Stepping out into the main room I took a deep breath and let it out, let my eyes rove casually, easily. The maids here did a good job. I pulled drawers out. When I got to the bottom one I reached under it and released the latch, sliding it all the way out to check and see if anything had slipped over one of the drawers and fallen behind. Maids never clean back there. I found a woman's scrunchy and two socks, but they could be anyone's. At least now I knew where missing socks end up in hotels.

I got down on my belly and searched under and around the beds. I lifted mattresses and looked in between. The whole room was cleaner than my mother's kitchen, which is saying a lot. The only good thing I realized from this trip was that the maids kept the damn place so clean that I wouldn't hesitate to recommend it to friends.

I went down to the front desk. There were two clerks behind the counter, one man and one woman. The man was older and balding with a very shiny pate. He was clean cut and pleasant looking. The woman looked to be about twenty two, had long stringy hair, several face piercings and looked to be anorexic.

I asked the two clerks if either one of them had been working the nightshift night before last. They both had. I asked them if they remembered the man who rented the room or anyone going up to it. The one thing they did remember was getting a phone call from room 509 at about 3:00 in the morning complaining about the noise from 511 and that it sounded like someone might be getting hurt in there. They sent someone up to inquire. The man who rented the room answered and apologized and said they were just having a good time and would be quieter.

I asked the clerks if they recognized Jonathan. They said he checks in about once a week.

"Do you usually get complaints from other patrons about him being noisy?"

"Rarely, but sometimes. We all have guessed that he is meeting here to have affairs or whatever. But then hey, this is Washington."

"Did you see a pretty blonde, blue-eyed, between 17 and 22 that came in?"

"I know who you mean," the pierced lady said. "She always comes in on the nights Mr. Spurrier checks in. We figured she was the one."

"What can you tell me about her?" I asked.

"Very pretty, dresses very boho, ya know, necklaces, bling, wears very low cut shirts that show her bra, tight short skirts, has curly hair sometimes, sometimes straight, always wears it differently, seems like a free spirit. To be honest, she looks like a hooker."

"Huh, well, some people do," I said. "What kind of personality does she have?"

"She usually smiles and says hi when she comes in. She seems nice, you know friendly, but not talkative." The pierced lady stated.

"Do you remember seeing her leave?"

"I do." The bald man said.

"Did she have anything with her?"

"She did. She always comes in with a shoulder bag. But this time when she left she was also carrying a briefcase."

"Did she go out the front door?"

"She did."

"How was she acting?"

"She just hurried out. She did stop at the door, set the briefcase down and looked through her purse. She mumbled and cursed to herself, like she couldn't find something. I asked her if she needed any help. She just looked at me and bolted."

"Do you remember what time that was?"

"About 4:30 a.m."

"Okay, thank you very much."

Now I had a time and I had Charlotte with the briefcase. It all fit very nicely with Jonathan's account.

I went home, poured myself a nice glass of tawny port and sat down and jotted things down on sticky notes. One wall of my apartment has two corkboards and one chalk board, which I use to post data and chalk out questions or thoughts I need to ponder as I work through a case. I went up to one board and stuck the notes up with push pins, stood back and took a sip of port. It was cold and velvety.

I had my first real data. Two witnesses placing Jonathan and Charlotte at the hotel and confirmation that they were regulars. I had a description of Charlotte and that she left alone with the briefcase. The game was afoot.

Chapter 7

The next morning I got up, shaved, had coffee and headed out to talk with Spurrier's wife. She didn't work and Spurrier told me she slept in late every morning. I decided to surprise her at 9:00 a.m. Jonathan told me that she always got up at that time to start her day. Catching people early in the morning in their homes, or other places where they feel safe tends to catch them when they are less distracted, less angry and distrustful.

Their home was in Georgetown. Some parts of Georgetown have 200 year old row houses and estates dating back almost to colonial times, surrounded by gardens in deep shade which look like the owners downloaded their gardens straight out of Better Homes and

Gardens Magazine. This was one of those homes. The house sat back one block off of Wisconsin Avenue. It was a three story brick home.

When I banged on the front door a small Latino lady who was about thirty years old answered the door. She had long beautiful black hair and sparkling dark eyes. I wondered if Spurrier had slept with her too.

"Hola, may……I…….hep…….you senor?"

"Hi, I'm Detective Goulet. May I please speak with Mrs. Spurrier."

"Oh…….she no Mrs. Spurrier……She a Senora DeManthe."

"Oh, well then can I please speak to Ms. DeManthe?"

"Si, I get her."

I stepped into the front hallway. The hallway I was standing in had a fifteen foot high ceiling with a crystal chandelier that created a hundred little prisms on the wall as the morning sun touched it. I was staring at the little prisms, thinking about how it would suck to see those when you woke up with a hangover when a woman breezed into the room who looked to be in her early thirties. She was stunning. She had dirty blonde hair which she wore with straight bangs across the front and let it hang straight down in back.   She had big brown eyes that were large and luminous, glistening and alive.

They tilted downward at the edges, giving them a slightly sad and seductive look that made you want to take her in your arms and tell her everything was alright. They were bedroom eyes, sad but hypnotizing. Her body was athletic, broad shoulders and a thin waist. She had breasts that looked clearly enhanced, though I'm not complaining. She was easy on the eyes. When she came into the room she was wearing a white bathrobe and there didn't appear to be anything underneath.

"Hi, I'm Lily, may I help you?" She extended her hand as she approached.

"Hi, I'm Frank Goulet. You're husband hired me."

She took my hand in hers and held onto it. "Oh yes, the private dick," she said in a huskier tone.

I've heard that one at least two dozen times and it never loses its lack of originality, even when said in a sexy voice.

"Do you mind if we talk?" I asked.

"Not at all." She smiled and stared up into my eyes. "Maria," she called out, never looking away from me. "Maria, Mr. Goulet will be joining me for coffee."

"Si senora," I heard from another room.

"Why don't you come with me and we can get more comfortable in the other room."

She turned and started to float away, swaying gently toward a door on the other side of the hallway. Her movements in that robe, with her long hair hanging down and her body moving so seductively made me feel like I was being lured into a Marlene Detriech movie and when we passed through the door ahead we would be stepping into a silent black and white film, devoid of words and color and it would be chic and classy, and she would light a cigarette that would be on one of those extended cigarette holders and all of our words would be printed on the screen beneath our feet so that the only way I would get any answers out of her was to constantly stare down at the bottom of the screen and read what she was saying and I knew I wouldn't be able to do that because it would be so hard to look away from those gorgeous eyes.

We stepped through the doorway into a long hallway. The ceiling was ten feet high and the walls were lined with oil paintings surrounded by antique frames. The paintings were a mixture of impressionist and realist landscapes along with a few pieces of modern art. I recognized one and paused to look.

"Is that a Thiebaud?"

Marlene paused and turned around in a sweeping gesture. She moved up beside me, surprisingly close, her breast touching my elbow. I didn't know whether I should move it or leave it and see what she did. It felt nice, so I figured what the hell and left it. I could smell the fragrance of her body mixed with some soft perfume she was wearing. It was distracting.

"It is a Thiebaud. I bought it for the house at auction. Are you an art fan?"

"I am."

"Goulet, is that French?"

"It's Chinese. My family is pure Mandarin."

"Cute," she countered, without missing a beat and turned to stare up at me. She stared at me a long moment, "Definitely cute."

I didn't dare turn to meet her gaze. "Are you the art connoisseur or is it your husband?"

She laughed a genuine heartfelt laugh, pulled back slightly from my elbow and looked up at me. "Jonathan, an art connoisseur? Hahahaha," she chuckled with real mirth. She slipped her arm more tightly around mine and for the first time I didn't feel like she was flirting or inten-tionally being distracting anymore. She simply took my arm and stood close. She stared up at the painting and chuckled again.

"No, no, Mr. Goulet, I buy the art for me. I graduated with a minor in art from college. My husband lets me buy art because he can show off the paintings and let everyone know that he owns original artworks from great artists."

"Wow, an original Thiebaud," I said, staring up at the work with genuine admiration.

It was a large painting of a street scene in San Francisco. In classic Thiebaud fashion the buildings stood along streets that were so precipitously steep that they looked more like cliffs, yet it all seemed to portray the steepness of the San Francisco landscape so accurately. I have been a huge Thiebaud fan for years.

"I've always felt like his style and works are inimitable. His work in unlike anything anyone else does. They are so unique and fresh," I said as I stared up at it.

She hugged my arm slightly in the friendliest way. "Hm, I feel exactly the same way."

After a moment she said, "Do you want to see some other originals?"

I looked down into her eyes. Those brown, moist bedroom eyes had a sparkle in them now that was lighter and more radiant and even more seductive. It made me wonder if she was conscious of being so alluring or if she was just that way by nature. I smiled down at her. "I'd love to."

She was a different person now. Her coquettish side was toned down and she led me around the house still holding her arm through mine. It was as if we were old friends or lovers. With her it was hard to tell which.

In the hallway there were well known artists like Warhol and Thiebaud and a Childe Hassam watercolor. And there were a dozen lesser known modern artists. When we entered the library was when I saw the paintings that surprised me. She owned three Bogdanoves. They were all dark and stormy paintings of the coast of Monhegan Island in Maine. The paint was thick and the churning feeling of the waves crashing into the rocks was palpable and almost gave you an involuntary shiver as you stared at them.

Lily felt me shiver slightly and she looked up at me again and hugged my arm closer. "Are you a Bogdanove fan?"

I never looked at her but just stood transfixed on the paintings before me. "I love Bogdanove. God that man captured the storminess of the sea and the coastline in a way that was so real you can almost feel the sea spray."

"I love Bogdanove too," she said, staring back at the paintings and hugging me more tightly, as if huddling closer for warmth. We stood silently staring at the paintings a long time.

At some point I turned and looked down into her face. She continued to stare at one of the paintings, lost at sea somewhere in her mind.

"Ms DeManthe, do you mind if I ask you a personal question?"

"Only if you call me Lily." She squeezed my arm gently.

I smiled. "Lily, why are you married to Jonathan?"

Something in her eyes changed. The sad

downturned corners seemed more pronounced and she stared back up at the Bogdanoves. I realized at that moment why she loved those paintings so much.

"That's a long story," she said.

"Well, your husband is paying me by the hour and it is an outrageous amount of money, so the longer your story is the more I'll get paid."

She smiled and looked back up at me, the playful coquette returned from the sea. She squeezed my arm. "Let's go have coffee."

Chapter 8

　　　We went into a large solarium that was attached to the back of the house. It was exotic with tall tropical plants and vines that stretched between trees and colorful bromeliads sticking up out of the crotches of the trees and along some of the larger branches. There were several colorful tropical birds that flew about higher in the greenhouse and there was a small stream that flowed, tumbling first down an eight foot waterfall before it began its meandering course through the stone floor of the solarium. Lily led me by the arm to the center of the room where there was a large bistro style table and some outdoor lawn chairs with large waterproof cushions. She released me from her grasp and moved around the table to the far side. I moved around the table and pulled her chair out for her. She looked surprised, said thank you and took a seat.

I returned to my chair opposite her. Maria was there in an instant with a tray with a large French press, two empty mugs, and a bowl of sugar and a small porcelain pitcher of crème. Lily said thank you to her. Maria smiled and left the room.

There was something that seemed very out of place about Lily surrounded by this opulence. I could see it in her when she thanked Maria. It was genuine and heartfelt, like one working class person to another.

I offered to pour her a cup of coffee. She accepted. She watched me pour and those seductive eyes of hers returned. She watched my hands.

"You have strong hands," she said softly.

"Their good for pouring coffee and I never spill a beer."

She smiled and took her cup from me, lifted it to her lips and sipped it black. I had figured her for a Splenda or Stevia kind of person.

I poured some crème into my own coffee and leaned back in my chair. A red and blue macaw flew overhead. When I looked back at Lily now she looked slightly older, the small crow's feet at the edges of her eyes gave away that fact that she wasn't in her twenties.

Obviously she tried to keep those appearances up, and at first glance it worked.

"How long have you two been married, nine, ten years?" I asked.

"Ten years, how did you know that?"

"The honeymoon has clearly been over a long time, and my hunch is Jonathan started scratching the seven year itch early. None the less, that would likely put it well up to at least six or seven years. But you mentioned you went to college and I am hypothesizing Jonathan married you shortly thereafter. Based on the fact that your age must be around thirty one or two, I would say you have been married ten years."

"And how in the world did you guess that Jonathan married me straight out of college?"

"It's more of a supposition really, but it seems clear he has a thing for younger women, so the likelihood that he would have been infatuated enough to marry anyone who was close to his own age seems very slight indeed."

"Do you tell fortunes too?" She asked.

"Only for criminals that I am tracking down. For them, it's pretty easy to read their fortunes. They'll spend many years in a big building surrounded by tall fences and living with other men all wearing bright orange suits."

She laughed. "Are you really a detective?"

"Of course, why?"

"I somehow tend to think of detectives as dour, with a paunch belly and pasty skin."

"I'm only dour when I'm served bad wine and I use olive oil on my skin. That's probably why you couldn't tell."

She chuckled and sipped her coffee. We both sat for a moment sipping and relaxing. She seemed completely at her ease now. I was debating how to phrase the next question when she suddenly made it easier for me.

"In case you're wondering, we sleep in separate bedrooms. He has, um, late nights with lady friends who stay over sometimes."

I sat staring at her, trying to comprehend how he could want anyone other than this gorgeous, classy woman who sat across from me.

"Surprised?" She asked.

"Dumbfounded."

"Oh, we still get it on. He comes in some nights and pops a Viagra and goes at it with me for an hour, sometimes two. It's a lot like a little horny Pekinese dry humping someone's leg. It's very romantic," she stated blandly.

"I can imagine."

"I doubt it," she said. She reached into the pocket of her bathrobe and pulled out a pack of cigarettes. "You mind?"

"Yes, but, if it makes you feel better, go ahead."

"You are direct aren't you?"

"I try to be."

She smiled. Her eyes became focused on the end of her cigarette and the lighter as she paused to light it. She set the lighter on the table, closed her eyes and inhaled deeply. Her lips parted and angled themselves to the side in a practiced manner as she blew out a long stream of smoke up and to the right.

"Did you ever smoke?" She asked.

"Gave it up ten years ago."

"I've given it up several times, but Jonathan drives me crazy and I find myself right back at it," she stated.

"Why don't you divorce him?"

"Hmmm," she chuckled, more to herself than to my question. She took another drag off the cigarette and blew the smoke out hard toward the ceiling.

"Have you ever been married Frank?"

"Once."

"Really? Hm, I guess I shouldn't be surprised. You're a handsome man. You probably have a lot of ladies interested."

"I'm afraid all the ladies who knock on my door these days are there to hire me to snoop on their cheating husbands."

"They would probably love a man like you to ease their pain."

"I fell for a client like that once. I'm a sucker for big sad eyes."

"Was she pretty?"

"Very."

"You have a girlfriend now?"

"Sort of. Maybe we should get back to why I came."

Lily narrowed her eyes and seductively wrapped her lips around the cigarette, drawing it slowly this time. Oh, she was dangerous. She blew out the smoke and said, "So tell me Frank, how can I help you retrieve my hubby's briefcase?"

"Do you know how it was stolen?"

She narrowed her eyes and her gaze took on a vitriolic stare, as if there was some thought in there she was burning holes through. "You mean, the hooker?"

"You know about that?"

She took another drag off her cigarette and blew it out hard. "He brings them home sometimes."

"Hookers?"

"Escorts, hookers, whatever. He humps practically any good looking woman that walks down the street. He picks them up, hires them……" Her voice trailed off.

I didn't know what to say so I waited.

"Did you ever fool around on your wife Frank?"

"I never did."

"You the loyal type?"

"I am."

"Believe it or not, I was at first." She took

another drag on her cigarette, held it in and released it. "Yes, I was the adoring little wife. Then he wanted to start having ménage a trois's. I didn't do it at first. I was a one man kind of gal. But he said he needed it. He said he loved me and that it wouldn't mean anything. He said a man's needs were different than a woman's."

She took another drag and then crushed out the cigarette in an ashtray. She took out another one and lit it.

"How'd you two meet?"

"I was a high school intern. I worked for his office because I wanted to study chemical engineering in college. His company does amazing things. God, when you're seventeen years old and a really handsome, really wealthy, really well known guy takes you out to expensive dinners and makes you feel so special…….." Her voice trailed off. She took another drag and let it out. "Then I worked for his office in my summers when I was home from college. I felt so special that he was so into me and thought I was so beautiful and smart."

"Is that when you two became romantic?"

She laughed. "Romantic? Hell he was banging me every chance he got. Yeah it was romantic."

There was a long silence.

"Please don't think badly of me Frank."

"Lily, you were a young woman, a kid. Hell, someone with his power and prestige and good looks, I'm sure it would have been hard for anyone your age to resist."

She laughed bitterly. "You know, he was married then. He took me home and we even did it while his wife was downstairs." She turned and looked me in the eyes. "I was brilliant, a really brilliant young woman and I fell for a bastard who was banging me while his poor wife was downstairs. I knew even then that he was sleeping with other women."

"Does he like to beat you up too?"

She didn't answer. There was a long pause while she took a deep slow drag and held it in. She let it out slowly.

"So, anyway, that's my little sob story." She snubbed out the butt in the ashtray.

"So why don't you divorce him now?"

"For what? I gave up everything after college for what I thought was the fairytale wedding. I moved in with him instead of following my dreams. Would I quit this just to meet some other man who will do the same damn thing? At least living here I can surround myself with nice things and good art and take long summer vacations to the Riviera."

"Why do you need any man? Go out on your own. You're smart and still young. Besides, not all men are like him Lily."

"I grew up in a household with an abusive father who cheated on my mother. Then I met Jonathan and thought I had it different. I feel like I've been looking for a good man most of my life and haven't been able to find one."

"The Marine Corps is always looking for a few good men. They find great ones all the time. Maybe you should talk to one of their recruiters."

She laughed.

"Give yourself a chance Lily. You deserve far better than Jonathan."

"What, someone like you Mr. Goulet?"

"Hell no, you would hate being with someone like me. I'm obsessive, never sleep, always working. I drove my ex crazy. Hell, I drive myself crazy. So, I don't blame her for leaving."

I took a moment to pour more coffee into each of our cups.

Lily got a faraway look in her eyes. "You know Jonathan grew up in a wealthy family. He had nannies and tutors and his own indoor basketball court for god's sake. His father taught him early on that money is power and the wealthy are the ones who really run this country, who make the rules. He lives in that wonderful world of the kind of people who float through life believing unwaveringly in themselves. The man has complete confidence in himself and when he walks into a room people feel that confidence and he is hard to resist. And he knows it. Hell, that's what I fell in love with. I thought he was the most charismatic man I ever met. He had it all."

I didn't know what to say. I studied her as she was lost in whatever realizations were going through her mind. She had real depth to her but it was buried deep beneath years of abuse and anger. She became aware I was watching her and she glanced my way. "Like I said, that's my little sob story."

"I'm sorry. Look Lily, I need to ask you a few other things."

"That's alright Frank. How else can I help you?"

"Do you have any idea who may have tried to sabotage your husband's business by stealing those plans?"

"No, but in a way, I hope they get away with it."

"My associate tells me SPURRIER AND FREEN could really suffer financially if this goes public."

"Good. It would serve that shit husband of mine right. I wish just for once his good charms and good looks and ego would bury him. He always seems to end up coming out smelling like roses, no matter what happens."

"Some people are like that."

"He sure is."

"When he arrived home after it happened, how was he, upset, distraught?"

"He was very calm. Jonathan is always very calm."

"He didn't seem upset?"

"He seemed upset in his own way, just deeply lost in thought and distracted."

"Did he tell you about it?"

"He did. He told me his briefcase had been stolen and he was worried."

We sat in silence. Maria appeared in the doorway carrying a tall glass with what appeared to be a bloody Mary on it. Lily saw me staring at it.

"It takes the edge off," she said.

"Sandpaper takes the edge off too."

"Well, around here there is always an edge that needs sanding Mr. Goulet."

She lifted the glass from the tray. I watched as she closed her eyes and took a long quaff. I looked around at the digs she was living in, thought of all the amazing artwork in her hallways, the maid who served her, and yet she has an edge on her life at 9:00 in the morning. All I could think about was Hemingway's To Have and Have Not. Boy did he nail it on the head about the skewed perspective of "The Have's."

I got up from the table and walked over to where she was sitting. I leaned over and gave her a very gentle kiss on the cheek, then stepped back and gazed down at her.

"What was that for?" She asked.

"You looked like you could use it."

She smiled. I turned and left.

Chapter 9

Leaving the Spurrier's home I headed across the Potomac River into Virginia to meet with Ted Freen at SPURRIER AND FREEN. As I drove I thought about Lily. There was deep pain and resentment in her. She had given up her young adulthood for Jonathan and now she hid in her lavish home with her paintings and her booze. She seemed like someone spiraling downward out of control and headed for a train wreck. It made her potentially dangerous.

I pushed a Miles Davis CD into the MP3 Player. I needed some blues to relax me and clear my head. Miles was on the horn, Cannonball was on the alto sax, Coltrane on the tenor sax and Oscar Peterson was on the piano. They blared away their melancholy tones as I sped up the highway.

As my mind shifted I began looking forward to speaking with Ted alone since he tended to be a bit of a wall flower when Jonathan was around. I headed out Route 66 to the Chantilly area. People in traffic were weaving in and out and cutting each other off while they were preoccupied with their cell phones talking and surfing the internet. I took the exit for Route 50 West and passed four different strip malls, then turned right into a labyrinth of industrial buildings. I felt like a rat in a maze as I turned down one street and then another trying to figure out which streets connected to the one I needed. I finally found Henreddy Drive.

SPURRIER AND FREEN was in an inconspicuous building, blending in with 10,000 other industrial parks across Northern Virginia. By the front door there were some numbers denoting the street address and the word SPURRIER AND FREEN to let you know you weren't in one of the other 9,999 buildings in the region.

I went in the entrance where I found myself in a small waiting area with an unstaffed reception desk. There was some inexpensive furniture for guests to sit on while waiting and an end table with past issues of People Magazine and Sports Illustrated on it. One blank metal door led out of the room and there was a video camera mounted in the upper corner of the room facing the metal door that led to the rest of the building. Beside it was a scanner for passing an ID through to open the door.

I walked over and tried the metal door. It was locked. I waited for five minutes. No one appeared at the reception desk. There was a computer behind the counter and a telephone. I walked around the counter, lifted the phone and dialed the number for Ted Freen's office. He picked up on the first ring.

"Ted Freen," he answered.

"Ted, this is Frank. I'm in the reception area."

"I'll be right out."

In case the camera was actually secretly filming something that could end up on candid camera or YouTube I decided to be a good boy and not pull my underwear out of my butt crack, or scratch my balls or pick my nose. You never know where your little bad habits could end up being viewed these days.

True to his word, the metal door opened within sixty seconds. He had a big smile and opened the door wide and waited for me to enter. As I approached he extended his hand toward me.

Ted was dressed as impeccably now as he was for lunch. He carried himself very well, having an air of professionalism and class about him. Every hair was in place. His teeth were bright white and straight and his fingernails looked manicured. He was a very clean cut gentleman, yet, he didn't look sanitized or plastic the way Jonathan did.

As he took my hand he said, "Thanks for coming Frank. Sorry to keep you waiting."

"No problem. It's such a warm and cozy room."

"It is a bit austere, but we have few visitors other than some military and private contractors. Let's uh, start with a little tour and then you and I can sit down in my office and talk. First off, this is SPURRIER AND FREEN Laboratories. We do a lot of our R&D here, but we have a larger facility out in the Shenandoah Valley. We like to stay as near as we can to Washington, but some of the environmental issues dictates our processing be farther out of town."

"Okay. Well, show me around the laboratory then," I said.

The basic building was one floor with several laboratories. Ted was the Senior Research Engineer who ran everything. As we walked around he tossed around words like ceramic composites, fine-grained ceramic nanomaterials and colloidal precipitation synthesis and hybrid polymer nanocomposites. My brain was in a fog as I tried to take it all in.

He took me into the lab related to the particular research which was stolen which he described as their ceramic research on aerospace and nuclear applications. I met three fairly young scientists, all chemical engineers who worked on the particular research that was stolen. One of them was a very youthful looking Chinese man named Reggie Tsui. Another researcher was a very pretty, petite Indian woman named Nancy Dasgupta. Then there was an African American man who looked to be in his early thirties named Rupert Green. All three were nerdy as hell and affable. As we walked through the building there were several administrative staff sitting at desks working the keyboards on their computers and there were two security guards posted throughout the building who were packing Glocks in hip holsters. Ted assured me that the employees in the other laboratories did not have access to this lab or to the safes where this material was kept.

The labs and hallways had no windows. There was a break room with 4 bright green 3' x 6' tables with chairs around them and there was some couches and chairs with bright orange vinyl cushions. The whole thing seemed a little garish considering everything else in the building was so bland, but what the hell do I know? Personally, I think the place would have driven me to drink heavily, but then I am always looking for a good excuse to do that anyway.

After the tour Ted showed me into his office. It was large. The walls were nicely painted a sky blue and there were many photos of sailboats on the walls and a shelf with three trophies on it. There was a gorgeous mahogany desk and a matching chair. Filing cabinets stood at attention in a perfect line along one wall as if awaiting inspection. There were three different safes along another wall. A large bay window behind his desk looked out onto a small lawn area with three Bradford pear trees growing there and two picnic tables under them. There was another group of industrial buildings about 150 yards away, directly across the grassy area. They were identical in color, size and shape.

Ted offered me some coffee. I accepted. While he poured it I gravitated over to the photos of the sailboats and the shelf of trophies. I could see Ted in several of the photos. The trophies were for sailboat races. He was a hardcore sailor. It definitely fit his style and personality.

Ted set two mugs of coffee on his desk and waited for me. I was enjoying the photos so I took my time.

He spoke from across the room. "Yeah, you guessed it right when you met me Frank. Sailing has been a hobby of mine since college days in California."

"Looks like more than a hobby, more like a passion. These boats are gorgeous. They all yours?"

"Yeah, at different times. The one on the

far left is my current boat."

I moved to the left and looked at the photos. It was a gorgeous vessel, clean, streamlined and sleek, much like Ted. In one photo you could see Ted standing on board in blue deck shoes, and wearing nice shorts and a polo shirt. A much younger woman was with him and in the background was steep terrain covered with stone white washed buildings that were stacked on top of one another as they clung to the nearly vertical mountainside.

"Where is this?" I asked, pointing at the photo.

"Amalfi."

"It's gorgeous. I've heard of it, but never been there."

"It is gorgeous. It's heaven."

"Beautiful boat."

"She's a Beneteau 57."

"Wow, 57 feet long?"

"Yeah, it's a nice comfortable size for living aboard."

"I can imagine."

"She's only five years old. I keep her in the Mediterranean, fly over a couple of times a year and do some cruising."

"Is that your daughter in the photo?" I asked wryly.

"Hardly."

"She Italian?"

"She is. I hope I can retire over there

before too long."

"With her?"

"Or someone like her."

"Amalfi, that's not far from the Campania wine region," I stated.

"Yes, yes that's correct," he said, seeming amused. "Are you a wine connoisseur?"

"More of an enthusiast."

"Ah yes, I guess most people who are true connoisseurs call themselves that. Are you familiar with Lacryma Christi?"

"Ah yes, the Tears of Christ. It's a great white wine, very nice." I continued to stare at the photos as I answered, trying to imagine myself on a boat like that, on that coast, sipping a glass of The Tears of Christ, standing next to that gorgeous Italian woman.

"I'm impressed. You do know your wines."

"I keep a copy of the Wine Bible on my bedside table."

"Hm, sounds like it's your religion. By the way, here's your coffee," Ted said.

"Oh, yes, thank you."

I suddenly remembered where we were and why I was here. I walked over to the desk, picked up my coffee mug and then took a seat across from him. Ted sat down as well. I took a sip of the coffee. It was bitter and tasted like whatever the cheapest discount brand was at the store. I set the cup down. I would get a good cup somewhere else later.

"So, you've been sailing a long time."

"Yes, sailing is big in California."

"And you and Jonathan met in college?"

"We did. Jonathan was a sort of larger than life character. He was brilliant, a total playboy, studied as little as he needed to, spent most of his time out getting laid or drunk."

"He's really that smart?"

"He's brilliant. Don't get me wrong, it's not like he didn't work when he needed to. Nobody coasts through MIT. But Jonathan didn't worry about being at the top of his class. He did enough to get by and the rest was all one big party. He's very competitive, always has to be the best. He refuses to fail at anything. You should see him play chess. Honestly, he is one of the best chest players I've ever seen. In college he played all the time and nobody could touch him."

"Refuses to fail?"

"It's true. He's the kind of man who you never want to play chicken with. He would die rather than lose."

"Sounds like there's an issue with ego."

"It's what makes him so successful."

"How about you?"

"I worked my butt off to get through Stanford."

"You like your work here?"

"I love it. It's all cutting edge research."

"So, how is working with Jonathan? Does he do much of the research?"

"Oh no, I mean, he and I founded the company. He has a creative mind and comes up with lots of concepts, but he is more conceptual and creative. The real day to day research is carried out here."

"Which is why you're here and he works in DC."

"Well, you need someone who can sell it, who understands the big picture and can talk to generals and politicians and scientists all in one. Jonathan could sell a truck load of satanic bibles to a Baptist minister. He's that charming."

"Jonathan sounds like someone who has always just kind of had things fall into his lap."

"It's true. He is one of those rare people who has it all, never really had to work terribly hard for anything."

"So you really spearhead the research and development and Jonathan sells what you make?"

"That's oversimplifying. Jonathan is very much involved in development. He knows the research and comes out here several times a week to brainstorm the data, review status reports and participate in R&D."

"Does he sleep with Nancy Dasgupta who works in the lab?"

"I really don't know," Ted said, looking suddenly uncomfortable.

"You really don't know?"

"I don't know," he said, looking me directly in the eyes now. "How is that relevant to our documents being recovered?"

"Until we know what happened everything is relevant to it," I countered. "I've noticed that all women who work for him or he is married to are all drop dead gorgeous. Does he pretty much sleep with everyone who works for him?"

"No, he doesn't. And as for the women we have hired over the years, we interviewed them and hired them together. And we have had some exceptionally brilliant women."

"I'm glad to hear it."

"Frank, I understand from Dani that you are an exceptional detective."

"I am."

"Well, if you don't mind me asking, you seem to be as focused on Jonathan's sexual life as you are on recovering the stolen documents."

"That's because it's his sexual life and habits that got you all into this mess in the first place and I am seeing a pattern here. Jonathan seems to have a long line of women he is always chasing after. Sex and chasing every skirt that breezes by don't typically fit too well with keeping tight security. Money and sex are the two easiest ways in the world to get people to give you pretty much anything you want. And when men can be tempted by sex their actions are very easy to anticipate. They can be manipulated like dogs on a leash. They say or do things based on what their little head is thinking instead of their big one."

"Well, Jonathan has always kept work and his indiscretions separate."

"You mean right up until his carelessness with a hooker got your secrets stolen?"

"Well it's one of his many little idiosyncrasies."

"Why is it powerful and rich people don't commit crimes when they steal company funds, or hump summer interns or pay to make people disappear? They only commit indiscretions or have idiosyncrasies."

"Well Jonathan is a man with rather large appetites. He has an ebullient personality, a lust for life. That lust spills over into other areas. That same passion and lust is what drives him to great success," Ted said.

All I could think while looking at Ted was that he should tattoo the word "minion" across his forehead.

I responded, "Well his ebullient lust for life maybe the downfall of this company. In case you're not up on your history books the same thing happened to the Roman Empire. You are part owner of this company Ted, how is it you can look right past his wanton behavior?"

"I owe Jonathan a lot."

I sat studying Ted. He began to get

uncomfortable. Finally he said, "Are we through?"

"Apparently," I replied.

Ted directed me to the files in his office. He gave me access to the personnel files of Reggie Tsui, Nancy Dasgupta and Rupert Green. Reggie piqued my interest. His family was Chinese. His parents still lived there. There was virtually nothing about his family ties, etc.

"Ted, Reggie has close ties to China. I don't see anything about his background check going into any depth."

"I know him personally. His family is trustworthy. His father works on the space program over there.   I have worked with his Father quite a bit."

I stared at him. "You are working on government contracts with high level security and you didn't do a more thorough background investigation on a man who has close ties to China? And to their space program no less? Ted, I don't give a shit if he is your gay lover and the two of you get it on every day at lunch time. This man has close ties to China. You know, China, one of the next big nuclear superpowers?"

"He's okay, I'm telling you. Trust me on this one. I know Reggie. He's good."

"How the hell did you all get clearance for your company and these contracts? What the hell do you do use Foo Chu fortune telling sticks to see who should work for you?"

"Frank, really, we know what we're doing. We are damn good at it."

"Well, you have glaring holes in your security."

Ted shook his head and ignored me. He looked annoyed. It was becoming more and more obvious to me that Ted really did not like confrontation. He was clearly the bitch in this relationship with Jonathan. It made me wonder if he tended to be submissive with all of his relationships.

I set Reggie's folder aside. I flipped through Nancy Disgupta's file. "India, they're a big nuclear country now too. Any unusual or suspicious behavior with Nancy?"

"No, she's quiet, keeps to herself."

I continued looking more deeply into the file drawer. I found a personnel file on a woman named Stella Buccino. She was a researcher who had been fired within the last eighteen months.

"Who's this employee, Stella Buccino?"

"She worked for us for five years. We let her go a little over a year ago."

"Why'd you let her go?"

"She was moonlighting, doing some consulting work for another company."

"A competitor?"

"Well, yes."

"Why didn't you mention her right off the bat?"

"She was working on something that was completely unrelated. Believe me, Stella wouldn't do something unethical."

"You fired her. You don't think there is a part of her that could be just a little bit happy to seek some retribution?"

"You don't know her. She is completely upstanding, brilliant, with a good career ahead of her."

"Was she involved in the R&D on the project that was stolen?"

"She was involved with the initial concept and the early aspects of development."

A little light went on somewhere in the corner of my dimly lit brain. "Who actually came up with the idea for this thermal barrier coating?"

Ted leaned back in his chair. Apparently a little light had come on in his head too. "Huh, actually, when I think about it, it was Stella."

"Does anyone here stay in touch with her?"

Ted paused to think. "I don't know. She wasn't terribly close to anyone here."

"Did Jonathan have a thing with her?"

Ted grew slightly red. "Yes, he did."

"Is it possible he still sees her from time to time?"

"No, I don't think he would do that."

"Is she pretty?"

"Uh, well, yes, she is."

Ted looked genuinely flustered and slightly flushed. A thought occurred to me. "Did you ever have a thing with her?"

"No, I didn't!" He stated emphatically.

I had hit a nerve.

I wrote down Stella's contact info and put her file away. While Ted wasn't paying attention I stuffed Reggie's file under my shirt, tucking it into my pants.

"Last question Ted, of the company's you are in competition with, what ones are most likely to do something like this?"

"Well, I honestly don't know. Perhaps Blue Light Industries, maybe Future Tech Engineering. I mean, they are also working on things similar. But, good luck in trying to prove that they would do something like this."

"Do you mind if I talk to anyone at those companies?"

"Well, I don't want it getting out that someone stole our research."

"I need to talk to them Ted to see if they had anything to do with it."

Ted acquiesced, but I could see he was nervous about it. As he wrote down the names and phone numbers of some people at those companies he pulled his top desk drawer open, extracted a large bottle of Tums and popped three or four of them into his mouth.

He gave me the names of four other companies and the names of the CEO's who ran them, as well as some of their leading scientists and engineers who were coordinating some of the projects they were working on. Then I thanked Ted for everything, including the coffee, even though it was unpalatable. We shook hands and I departed.

As I walked back to my car I felt like my brain was swimming in a sea of unsorted data and possibilities. There were numerous possible suspects now. Good investigative work is about being indefatigable in painstakingly looking through every possibility laid out before you. It's not the glamorous stuff on television shows. It's tedious work and requires dogged determination, forcing your mind to scrutinize lots of seemingly insignificant details until things start to slowly unfold.

As I sat down behind the steering wheel I realized that there were two things that were certain at this time. First, there were a lot of people and companies with possible motives to steal these documents. The question was how to begin narrowing down the field? The second thing which was certain was that I was in dire need of finding a good cup of coffee to wash the taste of that crap out of my mouth which Ted had given me.

I started up my car and hoped like hell I could find a Starbuck's somewhere nearby.

Chapter 10

On my drive back to DC I decided to call Isa. She's the woman I see, not at regular intervals. We kind of help each other out professionally, enjoy each other's company, catch a movie together, watch baseball and sleep together at times. It's an odd relationship, but it works, kind of. She has one of the most analytical minds of anyone I know. She challenges me. She also laughs at my stupid jokes and has the most haunting eyes I have ever seen. She's great company. But neither one of us wants to get too close. We are both private and very guarded people. It's hard to explain. But she's damn good company.

I scrolled through my contact list and selected Isabelle. She picked up on the second ring.

"Hey there detective." Her voice is always bright and effervescent.

"Hey there lady. You put any bad guys behind bars today?"

"All kinds of bad guys, but none as bad as you." She sounded happy to hear from me.

I smiled.

"Where have you been Frank? I haven't heard from you in three weeks."

"I know. I've been really busy with some cases, you know how it is."

I could hear paper's shuffling around on the other end of the phone.

"Did I catch you at a bad time?" I asked.

"No, I'm sorry. It's this case we're putting together. It goes to trial a week from tomorrow."

"We never seem to have time do we?" I asked.

"I know. Have you missed me?"

"I really have." And I really did.

There was a long silence. I heard her flipping through more papers.

"I missed you too Frank."

"Did you? Did you just miss the good sex or did you miss my brilliant rapier wit?"

"I just missed the sex."

I laughed.

I could see her dark eyes in my mind. She had the darkest eyes I've ever seen, so alive and mysterious, like the dark ocean on a moonless night.

She spoke more seriously. "Why do we do this to each other?"

"I don't know why we do it. We're both dysfunctional as hell."

"I know. It's why we're good together."

I laughed again. "Sad but true."

"I know. It is sad. But the sex is good."

"It's great."

"Are you seeing anybody else?" She asked.

"No."

"Are you?"

"No."

There was a long pause. She seemed preoccupied. We are both people who work too damn much and always have too many things on our minds. Yet, we can sit together for long periods and not say a word and be perfectly content. We can walk hand in hand through an art gallery, both absorbed in our own thoughts as we look at what is on the walls and it just feels nice knowing the other one is there.

"Hey listen, I need to run something by you," I said.

"Okay, shoot."

"I have a new client, rich, powerful, sleazy."

"Sounds like my kind of guy."

"He does contracting work for the

military, had some documents pilfered by a hooker."

She started laughing.

I started laughing too. "I know, the oldest trick in the book right?"

"Just about. So what do you need Frank?"

"I just wanted to know if you have ever heard anything about him. His name is Jonathan Spurrier and his company is called SPURRIER AND FREEN."

"You just want to know if there is any dirt, any illegal connections, that kind of stuff?"

"Exactly."

"Okay, well, I'll do some asking around."

"Thanks babe."

I could hear her flipping through more papers.

"Hey listen, you're busy. I'm going to let you get back to putting bad guys behind bars."

"I know, sorry Frank."

"No, hey, you and me always know that about each other. And I wouldn't want you to ever change that."

"What's wrong with us Frank?"

"I don't know. We're screwed up."

"Do you really miss me?" She asked.

I let out a heavy sigh. "I really do Isa. I miss you one hell of a lot."

It sounded like she was smiling on the other end of the phone. It's the slight exhaling sound people do when they suddenly smile.

"I miss you too," she said softly.

"Maybe we should get together tonight for a glass of wine after you get off," I said.

"I can't. I really have to work on this stuff."

"I understand."

"Do you?"

"I do."

"You're the best Frank."

"I know."

She chuckled. "Alright, well I'll ask around about your sleazy client."

She made a kissing sound into the phone like she was sending one my way.

"Alright, Isa, I'll catch you later."

I hung up and thought about her a long moment as I drove on through traffic. Then I snapped myself back to reality and decided to call the escort service. I knew from being a cop that many of them were high class operations, and others were barely a step above the girls standing on a street corner in their gaudy high heels and miniskirts.

I dialed the number Spurrier had given me. I had been debating how to approach this, whether I should just go head on and see if I couldn't finesse the guy to talk to me and bargain with him, or whether to pretend I was hired by Spurrier's wife to investigate his whoring habits for a divorce case, or simply pretend I was a potential client. Since I had no idea what this pimp was going to be like, a class act, a dumbass, or a badass, I decided to be extemporaneous and wait until I had him on the phone so I could go with my gut at the time. It's not a failsafe way to go but until you have an inkling who you're dealing with it's not too bright to have a nice neat plan that you assume will work on anyone.

The phone rang four times.

"Yo," was the response on the other end.

"Uh, yes," my gut told me to go with nervous rich guy who has never done this kinda thing before. "Uh, ahem," I cleared my throat trying to sound nervous. "I read on your internet page that I might be able to uh, meet someone discreetly."

"Yo my man, you a cop?"

I tried to act surprised and nervous. "No, no, hell no, what is this?"

"I'm just axing. What choo looking fo my man?"

"Well, to be honest, I uh, I uh......."

"Yo dude, you wastin' my time. What choo need?"

"Someone who uh, you know likes to play rough." I tried to sound uncomfortable. "Uh, preferably blonde. I like them blonde and athletic."

"I got whatever you need my man, young or old, short or tall, thin or full figured, you know what I'm sayin'? Check out my website. The ones who like to play rough are Petra, Charlotte and Eva. Let me know which one you like and we can set it up."

"You know I'm not that picky, I just like blondes. Are any of them blonde?"

"Charlotte and Petra are both blondes, but Charlotte is not available at the moment? But Petra, she's Eastern European, sexy and exotic."

"Uh, okay, well then Petra is fine."

"You got it hoss. So, where do you want to meet her? Do you have a hotel or do you want her to come to your home?"

"Oh, well, I have stayed at The Modicum before. Is that place okay?"

"Yeah, The Modicum. When can you meet with her?"

"Uh, tomorrow night, like maybe uh, 8:30?"

"That's cool. Petra is free tomorrow night, so, 8:30 tomorrow night at The Modicum. I'll set you up real nice."

"That will be great, Mr. uh, who am I talking to?"

"The name is Dex. You can't miss me. I'll be parked right outside The Modicum in a red Caddie."

"Oh, okay."

"What is your name?"

"Oh, do I have to give you my name?"

"Are you jerking my chain? What's your name my man?"

"Okay, well, I uh, I'm Harry Stenser."

"Yo, good deal Mr. Harry Stenser."

"Okay, well, thank you very much Mr. Dex."

The line went dead.

Chapter 11

The drive back to Georgetown on I-66 was going against rush hour so I smiled as I looked at the bumper to bumper traffic in the lanes heading in the opposite direction. They weren't moving at all. In twenty minutes I was already nearing Rosslyn, and would be crossing the bridge soon to head back into DC and then Georgetown. I was feeling good. I went to the research lab feeling as lost as a preacher in a whorehouse and came out with two strong leads.

Crossing into DC on Memorial Bridge I threaded my way around the Lincoln Memorial and then headed north passed the Kennedy Center. The Potomac River was on my left. It was a dull opaque green. There were crew teams out on the river in their long wooden shells. The rowers were in perfect rhythm, sliding back and forth on their seats as they dug their oars into the water and gave long pulls. There is something calming about watching crew teams. As I continued on I looked up and saw the sky was clouding up again, suggesting we might be in for more rain. In another ten minutes I was cruising slowly through backstreets in Georgetown looking for any available spot to slip my GTi into. I found one.

It was time to clear my head and let the thoughts I was pondering filter out. Back in my apartment I stripped down and changed into my running shorts and shoes. There was a chill in the air and there was still a little light outside. I slipped down the staircase and headed one block over onto the C&O Canal. The Canal always has a certain feeling to it. It's like you are stepping back two hundred years in time. The giant stone blocks that make up the walls are weathered and have little plants growing out of the cracks in between. The chalky green water in the canal sits as still as glass, reflecting images of the buildings that line the canal and people who are walking on the roadways and bridges above, while you run, lost in thought along the hard packed stone path. The National Park Service runs the old canal boats during warmer weather, but during the cool months the path is mostly just maintained for walkers, runners and romantic couples out to stretch their legs.

My 44 year old legs are still strong and virile. I've always kept them in good shape through running, sparring and heavy bag work. I like to think of myself as a seasoned fighter, not an older one. I hold Randy Couture up as my all-time role model. Even though he is retired now, he fought in the heavyweight division defending his world title in UFC up until he retired at the age of like 47 or something. In my book there is no tougher man in the world than Randy Couture. Whenever I feel like skipping a run or the weight room or my heavy bag work, I just think of Couture and feel ashamed. That guy was still the most brutal wrecking machine on the planet at 47, god love him.

I started out slow to warm up. Some of the regulars were out on the path. A small male group of Georgetown University students ran by chatting the whole time they were running. Several males and females who looked to be young professionals passed by in the opposite direction. I nodded and waved at a few of them I recognized. Then after three quarters of a mile at a slow pace I kicked it up into third gear and and set a nice pace.   The damp March air filled my lungs as I sucked the air in and out in a steady rhythm. I left Georgetown behind me as I headed north, surrounded by woods that lined the towpath and a stream of cars on MacArthur

Boulevard on my right. Thoughts of the case floated through my mind as lightly as the breeze. I pushed on.

I wasn't happy with the way the case was going. I was feeling a bit like a blind man in the middle of Times Square, not knowing which way to turn or which noises to listen to. If this was more than a case of theft and I needed to investigate competitive companies or even countries then I was way out of my league. I figured the best I could do for now is focus on individuals Jonathan and Ted dealt with. The fact that Charlotte was the one who took the documents made her a key to this whole thing. Did she take it on her own or did someone pay her to do it? She was the most important link for me at this point.

By the time I turned and headed back into Georgetown the crepuscular light of evening had settled in and the lights of Georgetown glittered. I like to time my runs so I come back as the lights are coming on. I suppose it's the romantic in me. I never worry about thugs or weirdoes who might be on the canal because I always carry a small .357 magnum derringer in the small of my back when I run.

I finished my run by walking the last half mile. Back at the apartment I did a bunch of heavy bag work, running through drills and combinations of elbows, hooks, finger stabs, knees, edge of hand strikes, mercilessly attacking the 80 pound bag as if my life depended it. After thirty minutes of bag work my knuckles were sore and I was soaked to the bone in sweat.

Showered and cleaned up I grabbed my laptop and headed downstairs to the bar. They do a really good chili with piles of onions and cheese on top, perfect for damp March evenings.

When I stepped out into the bar the place was hopping. Fiona wasn't around, but one of her longtime waitresses was there named Rosalind. She saw me enter and waved from behind the bar. The woman is hard, never smiles, and her poofed up wavy brown hair floats around her head like a dark cloud. Thank goodness one booth was still open beside the windows. I set my laptop on the table and slid into the booth. Rosalind was at my elbow by the time my ass was settled on the cushion.

"Do you ever stop working Frank?" She asked.

"I only stop working for two things, to eat a good meal or if some beautiful woman like you seduces me into a night of frivolous sex."

"Well, you know that ain't happenin'."

"Well there you go. That's why I am always working."

She rolled her eyes and shook her head.

"You want some chili or something else?" She asked.

"Chili sounds good, extra onions and

cheese, and a good glass of red wine. Do you have a decent Tempranillo or Syrah back there?"

"I've got both."

"Let's do the Syrah then."

I was deeply ensconced in looking up info on Stella Buccino on the internet when Rosalind slid my wine and chili onto the table. I thanked her, took a sip of wine and pressed on.

Stella Buccino was well known in the field of rocket science. She was born in the Emilia Romagna region of Italy and came to the U.S. as a graduate student. She had a PhD in Plasma Physics and Fusion Technology and a Master's degree in Ceramic Technology. Judging from several on-line articles she had moved on well beyond SPURRIER AND FREEN and was working as a private consultant on technology for NASA to create a new rocket technology involving plasma and magnetic fields to create an engine that will take U.S. astronauts to Mars in half the time.

I decided to give Stella a call. I had her cell phone number from the file at SPURRIER AND FREEN. I pulled out my cell phone and punched in her number. She answered on the third ring.

"Hello?" There was no detectable accent.

"Hello, this is Frank Goulet. I'm a private detective investigating a theft of sensitive material from a company you used to work for, SPURRIER AND FREEN."

"A theft? I haven't worked for them for a year and a half. I doubt I would be much help to you."

Her voice was pleasant, relaxed, someone who seemed at their ease.

"I am trying to cover all my bases and I was hoping you could fill me in on a lot of background info on people as well as the history of the information that was taken."

"I'm sorry, I'm not sure I understand how I could really help."

"The information that was stolen related to an idea you had for thermal barrier coatings for turbofan engines."

"Hm, I was involved but I was only a part of a team who were working on it."

"Ted Freen said you came up with the concept."

"Ted? Well he would be nice enough to give credit where it's due. Yes, I was heavily involved in the initial research and design."

"Could we get together and talk? I wouldn't take up too much of your time."

Stella let out a long breath, clearly considering my question. "Look, we didn't part under the best of terms, at least not between Jonathan Spurrier and I. If they lost some of their research or somebody took it, well, to be honest, it serves them right."

"Why is that?"

"Because Jonathan Spurrier fired me

because he was intimidated by me being the lead on this breakthrough. I was outshining him and he always has to be center stage. So once he had enough to take off with it he fired me and continued the work with the rest of his researchers."

She stated all of this in an amazingly calm manner.

"You don't seem terribly upset about it," I noted.

"He's a jerk. I work with far better people than him now and I've moved on. I was angry as hell at first, but what are you going to do?"

God this woman was so together.

"That's a pretty Zen like attitude. Letting go of what has happened and focusing on what is before you," I commented.

"Look, I like Ted. I think he never agreed with Jonathan on his ethics, but he is loyal to Jonathan to a fault. For his sake I will meet with you. When did you want to meet?"

"When are you available?"

"Uh, I live in Rosslyn. I could meet this evening or tomorrow evening. I am out of town after that."

"How about I meet you in an hour?" I suggested.

"Well, I haven't eaten yet. How about…."

"Excuse me for cutting you off, but since you are nice enough to meet with me, how about we talk over dinner? I am charging it to

Jonathan Spurrier so at least you can get a little bit of satisfaction out of that."

She laughed. We arranged to meet at the restaurant at the top of the Kennedy Center. It is a gorgeous atmosphere looking out over DC and the Potomac River and it is located not far from either one of us.

I quickly paid Rosalind and took one bite of my chili. Shit it was good. Oh well.

I rushed upstairs, changed into a nicer shirt, added a bola with a turquoise bear track on it, threw on a silver Native American bracelet, my cowboy boots and my black leather jacket. Then I went out to my GTi and drove over to the Kennedy Center.

Chapter 12

I waited at the restaurant entrance. Stella arrived right on time. I recognized her from her photo. I waved as she approached. God she was stunning. She had long chocolate brown hair that was thick and bouncy like on those adds for shampoo. Her dark hair framed her face like a halo as she approached. The straight bangs across her forehead accentuated her large green eyes that were the color of jade and seemed to take in everything around her, like the eyes of a cat. She had high cheekbones and a small turned up nose that made her eyes stand out that much more boldly. She was nicely shaped with athletic legs and a very womanly gait as she approached, swaying ever so slightly from hip to hip. She dressed in a European style, with nicely fitting designer jeans and a large red sweater which contrasted with her dark hair. It was simple yet somehow classy. Her only makeup was bright red lipstick to go with her sweater. It was a nice touch.

I waved as she approached. She smiled and walked right at me. As she got within a few feet she extended her hand.

"I'm Stella."

"I'm Frank."

"Do you mind if I see some kind of identification?"

I pulled out my private investigator's license and also showed her my badge and explained I was a retired DC detective.

"Oh yes, I thought the name sounded familiar. I have read about you several times over the years for homicide cases you were involved in," she said, her eyes opening slightly as she realized this.

"That's me."

"You're French right?"

"My parents are and that's my lineage. I grew up in America."

"Where are they from in France?"

"My father was born in a town in Burgundy called Auxerre but he grew up in Paris. My mother was from Cantal in the Auvergne region. It's a region of ancient volcanos that nowadays produces great cheeses instead of lava beds. Shall we?" I asked, sweeping my arm forward to direct her into the restaurant.

We each went through the cafeteria style line and picked out various things to eat. The food there is good. I got a hot plate of beef burgundy, rice and grilled asparagus. Stella got eggplant parmesan. We both got a bottle of beer. There were quite a few people seated in the restaurant, no doubt eating before seeing whatever show they were here for tonight. They were dressed in a mix of formal attire and casual dress. I spotted a table in the corner beside a plate glass window and pointed it out. We threaded our way through the crowd and set our trays down.

I pulled her chair out for her and she looked up at me with her piercing green eyes. Wow. She thanked me and scooted up to the table.

As I sat down I said, "So you are from the Emilia Romagna region originally, correct?"

"Yes, I am."

"Your English is perfect, no accent."

"My mother is an American who moved to Italy when my parents married."

"Well you come from one of the greatest culinary regions in the world."

"I know. That is the single thing I miss the most. The cheeses, the wines, fresh olive oil and Balsamic vinegar. But, it's also why I became interested in ceramics. My family has produced traditional Italian pottery for over four hundred years. I grew up hanging out in my uncle's pottery workshop. I was such a nerd and wanted to understand it all more from the chemistry side of it."

"And now you create high tech ceramics for nuclear and aerodynamic applications."

"My ancestors never could have imagined what we do with ceramics now. My uncle has a hard time understanding how ceramics can be used to make missiles fly faster and how it protects space craft."

"So do you go back often to visit?"

"At least once a year during the holidays."

We both looked down at our plates and took a bite. As I did I glanced around at the people in the restaurant. "It's funny how a lot of people don't really dress up much anymore for the theater."

Stella glanced around. "Do you go to the theater much?"

"Whenever I can. I saw Kate Blanchette here last year in Uncle Vanya."

"Really?" She seemed genuinely surprised. "No offense but judging from your seventeen inch neck and scarred up knuckles I wouldn't have pictured you as the theater type."

"I read and cook good French meals too."

"Are you now updating your personal profile or are we here to talk about Spurrier and his stolen documents?"

"Ah, you're correct, and I apologize. I always find that investigations go easier if you break the ice and chitchat for a bit first."

"So you weren't coming on to me?"

"Perhaps unconsciously, but no, this is my normal pre-investigation banter."

"Well, your method must be effective as from what I have read you seem to always get your man."

"Or woman, let's not be sexist."

"Do you always get your person?"

"Not always, but usually."

"And modest," she noted.

"More like honest. There is always one who gets away."

"What is the most difficult case you ever worked on?" She asked, her eyes glistening with curiosity.

This was good. She was loosening up.

"Hm," I grunted in a thoughtful way. "The most difficult case? Well, I don't know about the most difficult, but maybe the most vexatious was nailing the killer who was stalking people along Independence Avenue."

"Oh, I remember that. That was you?"

"Well, it was me who investigated. It wasn't me who was the stalker."

She laughed. "You know what I mean."

I smiled.

"What was so vexatious about it?"

"I arrested him, got him off the street. A judge said the evidence was obtained illegally and set him free." I paused and took a sip of beer.

"What happened?"

I turned my head and gazed out the window. A light rain was beginning to fall on the terrace. Beyond the terrace I could see the Parisian style lights along Memorial Bridge and the flat dark surface of the Potomac River. On the Virginia shore, Lee's Mansion stood high on a hilltop. Its marble columns and stone walls standing like a ghostly image looking out on the world below. I continued to stare at it as I said, "He killed two teenagers."

"Oh, I'm sorry."

"Yeah, two teenagers, just being dumbass kids." As I spoke I could still see their faces in my mind, swollen, lacerated and bruised, bloody, barely recognizable.

"Were you able to arrest him for that?"

Still looking off into the distance I said, "I caught him."

"Were you able to convict him?"

"No, we didn't need to."

"I don't understand," Stella said, staring at me.

I didn't answer.

"Did the killer go free?" She asked.

She was persistent. Maybe that's why she was a good scientist. I realized I shouldn't have mentioned this case.

"Frank, did the killer go free?"

I looked at the raindrops splattering on the rooftop. The rain was falling harder. Small puddles were forming and the raindrops made tiny circles as they landed in them. I replied softly, lost in my memories. "I tracked him down and I shot him."

"You killed him?"

"I did."

"So, you just killed him?"

I didn't answer. I just continued looking out the window. Stella grew quiet. There was a long silence. I took a deep breath and watched the rain fall. The water on the roof glistened in the terrace lights.

"I'm sorry for bringing it up." She sounded sincere.

"No, I'm sorry. I don't usually discuss things like that except with police buddies." I turned and looked at her. "I have to say, you are very persistent in your line of questioning."

She smiled slightly, but her eyes looked sympathetic. "It must be hard dealing with things like that."

I looked down at my food. "Sometimes. It's always worse when kids are the victims."

I could feel Stella's eyes watching me. I really didn't want to meet her gaze so I moved food around on the plate with my fork and lifted a forkful to my lips. The sauce was rich. Stella took a bite of her eggplant parmesan. We both ate in silence for a few minutes. As I chewed I turned and looked out at the rain. At one point I felt her eyes upon me, studying me. I turned to look and she quickly averted her gaze out the window. I took another bite and looked outside again.

After a few minutes I turned to her and asked her questions about Spurrier, Freen, SPURRIER AND FREEN, their research and their contract. She seemed open with her answers. Finally, she said, "Look Frank, I find it hard to believe some country or company would steal their work."

"Why is that?"

"I don't think they have made any real progress on it since I was fired. There are other companies out there who are working just as hard with competitive research. So unless they have done something which Ted hasn't mentioned then I'm not sure they would be high on someone's list."

"Are you sure? You've been gone some time now. Maybe they have really advanced what they were doing."

"Maybe," she said. "But, I talk to Ted pretty regularly. We're good friends. And it sounds to me like they haven't taken it much Further than when I was there. This kind of research is very competitive and if they are dragging their feet, believe me, there are numerous companies who are pushing ahead."

"Really?" Now I was very interested.

"Don't get me wrong. I know people who would love to get their hands on the research. It's good work. And if they could really develop this new thermal barrier coating it means the missile engines could take much more heat and stress. That is significant. It would earn them an important new patent and many millions of dollars. But other people are working on things as well."

"You know Stella, Ted told me you weren't close to anyone there and that as far as he knew no one there stayed in touch with you."

She visibly recoiled, with a look of utter bewilderment. "What?"

"That's what he said."

She stared down at her plate. Her surprise was genuine. She stared down a long moment trying to digest what I just said.

"I'm, uh, I can't imagine why he would say that." She stumbled over her words.

"Did you ever have a thing with Jonathan or Ted?"

"Jonathan was always hitting on me. I think I seemed exotic to him. He took me out to dinner numerous times to talk about research. Ted always seemed kind of jealous."

"I hate to be nosey, but, did you and Jonathan…….?" I let my question trail off.

"Oh good god no," she blurted. "Hell no,

I would never sleep with that misogamist pig."

I don't know why but I was relieved to hear it.

"Do you think Ted thought you did?"

"Probably. He always looked like he had been slapped in the face every time I went out to dinner with Jonathan and would sulk and pout around the office the next day."

"Do you think Ted is the kind of guy who has been secretly holding a lot of resentment toward Joanthan?"

She looked at me. "Do you mean do I think Ted would sell their research or try to do something to discredit Jonathan?"

"Exactly."

"Ted would never do something like that. I mean, I'm sure he must be at least a little frustrated that Jonathan always steals all the credit for being the brains behind everything. But Ted just isn't the kind of person that is vindictive or even dishonest."

"You'd be surprised Stella. I have locked up little old ladies who poisoned their aging old husbands, and sweet little old men who strangled their elderly wives."

"Ooh, well, I just think you are barking up the wrong tree with Ted."

"It's important to consider every possibility," I said.

Stella took another bite of her food and she chewed for a few minutes, lost in thought.

"Well, as far as why Jonathan fired me, I know the real reason was because it hurt his male ego. I was the one woman he came on to at the office who just flat out said no. And, like I said earlier, I think he also felt a little more than intimidated by my research. I had to explain things to him sometimes more than once. I am not always very tactful like Ted is. Ted strokes Jonathan's ego. He always puts things delicately so Jonathan doesn't look bad. I never did that."

"Huh, this is very enlightening. The way Jonathan talks it sounds like they have the contract sealed up tight."

"No, no way," Stella said very matter-of-factly.

We finished our dinner and continued to chat about other things. Stella asked if we could take a walk on the terrace even though the rain was falling steady. I had an umbrella and we shared it. We walked over to the edge of the terrace and looked out over Memorial Bridge. The large statues on the ends were glistening in the rain as the Parisian style street lamps bathed them in a pinkish light.

Stella seemed totally at her ease as we spoke. She talked more in depth about Jonathan, Ted, Reggie and the others. Her opinions were illuminating. She didn't really understand why Reggie worked there. He was a smart man and had a good overall academic background, but she definitely had the feeling it was more of a favor to his family.

I asked her for information about the rival companies which Ted mentioned. Future Tech Engineering was the one Stella reacted to very quickly.

"Oh, I think they would be very interested in whatever SPURRIER AND FREEN had," she replied.

"But you said their research seemed stalled."

"Yes, but despite that, their lines of research are cleaner and they have better data than Future Tech."

"How is SPURRIER AND FREEN doing overall?"

"I think Jonathan did a lot to create the company and get it going, but he has become the rich playboy and the company is suffering."

"Do you think Ted or others might resent him for that?"

"Probably. Ted works really hard. He is very devoted. It must be hard to watch Jonathan be the one who always gets the credit."

"Are there others that might feel the same way?"

"Probably, Jonathan had a great company but he is becoming unfocused, not keeping up like he was. I'm sure there are investors and employees who are angry."

She finally said she needed to get back home. In the parking garage under the Kennedy

Center we parted ways. She said she had a good time. We shook hands and I told her I really appreciated her help.

I took my time driving home. I listened to the rain on my car roof and pondered her version of what was going on at SPURRIER AND FREEN.

Chapter 13

It was still raining as I drove home. I listened to the rhythm of the windshield wipers and stared out at the glistening lights of the city. I love the rain, but there are times it makes me feel too alone with my thoughts, too introverted.

As I drove on I pulled out my cell phone, scrolled my contact list and selected a number. The phone picked up on the fourth ring.

"Hi Frank," she said in a friendly tone.

"Hey Isa, what are you up to tonight?"

"I'm going over some briefs for tomorrow. What's up?" She always has such an easy going tone in her voice. You would never know she is one of the best Assistant D.A.'s in the federal court system.

"I was wondering if you had some time

tonight, you know?"

"Ooh, Frank, I hate when you do this to me off the cuff." I could imagine her biting the right side of her lip right now. She always does that when she is grappling with what she should do versus what she wants to do.

"Are you biting your lip right now?" I asked.

She laughed. "I hate when you do that too."

"Hey, they pay me to notice the little things you know? So, are you free?"

"What did you have in mind?" Her voice was deeper now, but quieter and playful. I knew she was biting her lip harder now.

"I have a really good bottle of Pouilly Fumé in the fridge and some fresh shrimp and cocktail sauce."

"Shit," she said.

"I figured we would eat in the bathtub, candlelight, a little Dexter Gordon or Cannonball Adderley, sip some wine, get you drunk, see if anyone's hands end up in inappropriate places."

"Oh, you bastard. I have got to finish going over these briefs. Why do you do this to me?"

Chapter 14

I had the bath nice and hot by the time she arrived. Her dark eyes were glistening when I opened the door. They are the eyes of a barred owl, black, shiny, expressive eyes that take in everything at once. She runs a lot outside and her cheeks always look slightly flushed and pink from the fresh air. She has long dark brown hair that she always wears in a long French braid. Her body is strong and muscular. Not big muscles, but rather a fighters muscles from years of practicing Muay Thai Kickboxing.

I answered the door in a towel. She didn't say a word, just came in, laid her legal briefs on the couch, slipped off her shirt and pants, and then slipped out of her satin lacey briefs, wiggling her cute bottom and shimmying them off to drop around her ankles.

God she looked sexy. I handed her a glass of cold Pouilly Fumé and we kissed softly.

"Only for a couple of hours," she said. "Then you are helping me with my briefs."

"I just helped you out of your briefs," I said with a smile, taking her hand and leading her back toward the bathroom.

"Is the shrimp fresh?"

"Would I give you anything other than fresh shrimp?"

She jerked on my hand, spinning me around. I spun and faced her. She let go of my hand and pulled my towel off, letting it drop to the floor. Our bodies were as naked as the day we were born.

"Come here you," she ordered, her eyes sparkling.

The bath had to wait.

I added hot water later and we ate the shrimp and listened to Cannonball. We made love in the tub and then again on the living room floor. She is as sexy and as smooth as a glass of Graham's 20 year Tawny Port.

She pulled on one of my big flannel shirts and I pulled on my sweats. I made coffee and we sat on the living room floor going over her files while the rain poured down on the roof and splattered on the windows. At one point she started yawning. She laid her head in my lap and made me promise not to let her sleep more than an hour. I stroked her hair.

As she was drifting off she said, "How come we don't ever do something more official Frank?"

She is so refreshingly direct, saying whatever is on her mind. I looked at her hair as I stroked it and thought about her question. I was tired, happy, a little tipsy. "We both suck at relationships and we're both workaholics."

She yawned. I continued stroking her hair.

"Do you think it would be different if either of us met the right person?" She asked, her voice sounding farther away.

I exhaled and thought about it. "I don't think so. You know, I met a woman, a suspect, who I had the best time talking to today. And after I talked to her all I could think about was you."

She never lifted her head, but in a sleepy voice said, "Was she was pretty?"

"Gorgeous."

"Prettier than me?"

"Not anywhere near as pretty as you."

She smiled softly and said, "Good."

I stared at my hand as I stroked her hair, mesmerized by it as if I was staring at a pendulum that had me hypnotized by its constant motion. Her hair felt so soft. Her face was so peaceful as she laid there.

She yawned, then said, "I think all those

years working the streets, seeing what you saw, maybe something inside you kinda closed down or died."

I thought about what she said. I thought of those two teenagers who died because of the judge's decision. I thought of dozens of bastards I had locked up who had no remorse after beating the brains out of their wives or husbands or some old person who they killed just to get their social security check. I remembered back to when I met Isa. I thought of the scum bags she tried like hell to lock up, murderers, rapists, total pieces of human excrement that should have been put away forever, but many of them were out walking around because of some technicality. One of them had come after her when his trial was over and came within an inch of killing her. I knew she understood why I am who I am, because I understood her for the same reason.

"Do you think that's true?" She asked.

"Probably."

She yawned again and slipped her hand over my thigh. It was the softest and simplest gesture, arousing, yet I didn't want to disturb it by moving. It was sweet. I leaned over and kissed her hair. It smelled like bathwater.

"Don't forget to wake me up," she whispered.

I smiled and watched my hand stroking her hair while I listened to the rain.

Chapter 15

After we had coffee in the morning Isa took a shower and headed back to her place to get ready for work. I was groggy but puttered around the apartment, sipping coffee and letting my head clear as I thought about where things stood with the case. I settled into my large overstuffed chair by the window and watched the slugs outside on the street below as they jostled around each other in the morning mist. I was damn glad I was up here enjoying my warm cup of joe.

Investigations always leave my mind with a million bits of information, most of it useless and you have to find a way to let it sort itself out. Being with Isa last night helped me to stop thinking about the case for a while. I felt more focused now. As I sat and stared at the rain my mind slowly sifted through the bits and pieces of the case. I didn't try to interpret them, just let the bits run by, like watching an old silent movie. I thought about Jonathan and Ted and Reggie and Stella and Lily and Nancy. Jonathan had really created a world which revolved around him. He was brilliant, not just academically. He was a person who had large appetites and knew how to get what he wanted.

He had men like Ted, who was clearly brilliant and organized and seemed to be the real glue that held the company together, yet waited on Jonathan like his little bitch. Lily, beautiful, smart, classy, looked like she should be one of the portraits hanging on her own walls, yet she was submissive and staying with Jonathan. The man had panache and charisma that people were attracted to. Dani even seemed enamored with him. The guy lived the way he wanted, did what he wanted and the world catered to him. I was building good profiles of the players who were involved on some level but I still didn't have a lot to go on. I had some good solid facts, but not enough that was substantial. I needed to just walk and let things rattle around and see if I could figure out what to do next.

I liked Stella a lot as a person. She was enjoyable to talk to. She certainly had motive but seemed unlikely. Ted Freen was another one who I liked at a gut level. He loved sailing, he was smart, and if I had to bet, I would guess on the water is where he really came alive, when he was away from people and not trying so hard to please them. But the one thing both of them had in common, they were brilliant, maybe more than I thought, and this is where gut instincts need to be handled delicately. Gut feelings should never be ignored, but they should never replace deduction and logic. Everyone one of these people were suspects.

I sipped my coffee. The rain ran down my window and I watched it erratically change course and head off in unpredictable ways. After a couple of refills of coffee I got up to check e-mails. There was one from Angel.

Haven't found dick. The dumpster was emptied, so I just searched any likely spots within six blocks. Nada.
Dogbone is setting up surveillance and should have everything up and running by tomorrow.
Angel

Angel always has such an elegant way of putting things. I wrote him back and told him to hold tight for now and I would call him later in the morning.

Chapter 16

I got up and showered, went downstairs to the bar and had some eggs, bacon and toast. I quickly threw on some clean clothes and headed out to an appointment with an old friend. At the District Station I went up the stairs and down a hall. The words Vice Unit were stenciled onto the glass pane of one of the doors. As I passed through the double doors I saw the face I was looking for.

"Hey there lady," I said.

Tina smiled at me, her wizened old eyes crinkling up at the edges. "Why look who it is, the legend himself."

I walked straight to her desk, which was stacked high all around her with papers, files, reports and 8 x 10 photos. Tina had an ageless kind of face. Her dark brown skin was as smooth as a lake on a windless day. She was petite and smart. Those wizened old eyes of hers, which had seen things people really shouldn't be exposed to, were sagacious eyes, giving her a kind of Yoda quality. They were eyes that always had a hint of a smile, which she was beaming at me as I approached. I came around her desk, leaned in and gave her a big kiss on the cheek.

"Ooh, look at you, buttering me up with a kiss," she said.

"Well, now that I'm retired I can get away with that. If I had done that while we were working together I might have been canned for sexual misconduct."

"I hear you're still dating that Assistant D.A."

"Not dating, we're just friends."

"Friends? I guess very good friends from what I hear."

"It's not like that."

She smiled. "So Frank, how is the private sector?"

"It's liberating, cuts out a lot of red tape."

"Must be nice. So what can I do you for Frank?"

I sat down on the other side of her desk. "I have a very rich client who has been playing around with some ladies of the night."

"Why do they do that?"

"It's one of life's great mysteries. But, I am looking for a specific young lady he has had relations with who stole something from my client, which he really needs back."

"Imagine that, a dishonest hooker. What is happening in the world today, huh?"

"I know. What happened to the good ole days when an honest John could fall in love with an honest lady of the night who would turn her money over to her honest pimp?"

"Were there ever days like that?"

"Well in the children's stories my mother used to read to me at bedtime all the hookers and pimps were honest and gave half of what they earned to charity."

Tina shook her head. "You are bad, you know that?"

"That's what my ex always says. Hey listen, my client, named Jonathan Spurrier, has committed what he calls 'an indiscretion' with this little young thing and she took him for more than her hourly rate. Her name is Charlotte. She's between 17 to 18, blonde, blue-eyed, athletic, uses a pimp named Dexter Deahl who advertises an escort service on the internet called All Your Needs Escorts."

"Huh, very original."

"I thought so. I looked on their website and found her listed as twenty two years old."

"Maybe she is twenty two."

"Not according to my client."

"Well, I have heard of that escort service. There's a lot of those operating now. You know Virginia and D.C. combined is one of the very worst regions in the nation for human trafficking, especially for trafficking minors. They still use clubs, but a lot more of these escort services are popping up. Most of these services will meet people at their hotels or home. Some of them have clubs you can visit. They're slick, usually make a big point out of saying that they don't engage in prostitution and that it is illegal. They claim they offer massages, body rubs and adult entertainment."

"You nailed it right on the head."

"Sure is different from the old days when the street walkers stood out on streets in their tiny skirts and high heels. These pimps got smart when we started booting their asses off of the D.C. streets. We hit 'em hard and cleaned up 14th Street. But, they just raised their game and started advertising more on the internet. It's smart. They make more money and deal with higher classer clients, at least some of the time."

"You just gotta love that kind of entrepreneurial spirit, you know?"

"Yeah, it ran all those little hourly room rate motels out of business," Tina said.

"Imagine how many poor little STD microbes lost their homes when those places were demoed. I hated going into those places to bust people. The floor always seemed sticky and

I felt like I needed to wear a hazmat suit."

"You and me both. Well listen Frank, I'm not really sure how I can help you."

"I just need to know whatever you've got about this escort service, this hooker who goes by Charlotte or the pimp who runs the service. Anything would be helpful."

"Well, as far as the escort service you named the only thing I really know about them is that they stay pretty clean, they tend to cater to some pretty high class clients on Capitol Hill. It's actually run by a woman named Xavier, who usually deals with the high class clientele like Senators and diplomats. She's organized, a good business woman. That pimp you mentioned takes care of all the outcalls and enforcing. Dexter Deahl acts and talks like a low class pimp but he's smart. He's the one man the clients deal with directly. He's tough. That's why Xavier lets him deal with them. But it's also so she can run the massage parlor and keep her rep a little further from the outcalls in case the girls get nailed for anything illegal. If the shit goes down she can say Dex must have been having them do it on the side."

"She sounds pretty savvy. You ever catch any word of her girls ripping anybody off?"

"Nope, but then, who knows how many people report that kind of thing. They don't really want the police involved most of the time. In fact, your client is a case in point. He hired you instead of coming to the police."

"Exactly. But, the fact that you haven't heard scuttlebutt on the street about Xavier's girls ripping people off probably means they don't make a habit of it."

"Actually she deals in both men and women. But no, she seems to keep it pretty clean. She deals with very high paying clients on Capitol Hill, CEO's, high-class Washington affairs. She's smart enough to know that you don't keep those clients if your girls or boys are ripping them off."

"Does this pimp have a rap sheet?"

"Oh yeah, he's got classic stuff like pimping, possession of firearms, assault, felonious assault, etc. But he is very savvy, like a lot of them are."

"Savvy enough to plan something more elaborate?"

"Hey, you know the streets even better than I do. You got guys who dropped out of middle school who are driving Escalades and running crack houses, pimping, fencing stolen goods. I mean, some of these guys know more about getting around the system than you and me know about how to operate within it."

"I hear you. So is The Modicum used for hooking very much?"

"Not anymore more than any other decent hotels in D.C. The escorts will meet people anywhere."

"So the hotels are not necessarily collaborating with the escorts?"

"No, the nice hotels don't want any part of that. Look, it's smart for these services to use nice hotels. The management doesn't really know if someone has a guest in. And what people do behind closed doors at decent hotels is their own business. D.C. is filled with lonely, visiting diplomats and lobbyists, a long way from their upper middle class wives and hubbies. Nothing takes the loneliness out of a business trip like a discreet warm body. And some of these companies and lobby groups keep people like Dexter Deahl and Xavier on speed dial so their visiting clients can be kept happy."

"I guess a lot of politicians and businessmen are just a bunch of prostitutes anyway, so they probably feel right at home using these services. I know my client, Jonathan Spurrier sure does."

"Well, this is D.C. It's all about power and money and doing whatever it takes. Some of the hookers make a lot of money. Some of them do it totally because they like doing it, and other ones get coerced, brutalized, hooked on drugs or enslaved into it. It's a very seedy world they live in and the pimps are the real scumbags in all this. Dexter Deahl is out at the head of the list of scumbags."

"Alright Tina, well, I'm supposed to meet up with Dexter and his girl Petra tonight. He said Charlotte wasn't available, so I figured I can pay Petra for information and see what Dex knows."

"You be really careful with Dexter Deahl Frank. The word is he came from the gutters of New York and he has been implicated in the disappearance of several hookers who may have ripped off Xavier or her clients. So if your young lady Charlotte was acting on her own it may well be that her vacation is a permanent one. You watch yourself with Dexter Deahl."

I smiled. "Actually Angel will be talking to him."

"Oh good lord, I don't want to find pieces of Dexter Deahl floating in the Potomac tomorrow morning."

"Angel will be very discerning in his approach."

"Yeah, like a damn bull in a china shop. Frank, seriously, you tell Angel what I said, no dead bodies or severed body parts."

I continued to smile. "I'll see what I can do."

I walked around the desk and gave Tina another peck on the cheek. She shook her head back and forth and said, "Get the hell out of here."

Chapter 17

I met with Reggie Tsui for lunch. He lived in Arlington and he left work early to meet me. We met at a burger joint on Wilson Boulevard called Rita's Original Burger. It's a gourmet burger joint that does some remarkable things with a patty of beef. I was sitting at a booth having a Corona when Reggie bee bopped in. He is hip, walks with a bounce to his step. His hair is short and black, sticking straight up like the old military style haircuts. He was wearing camo pants, a black North Face jacket and had headphones draped around his neck. He paused just inside the doorway and scanned the room. I waved him over. His mouth erupted into a big toothy smile as he headed over my way.

He stuck out his hand as he approached. "Hi Frank."

"It's good to see you again Reggie. Thanks for meeting with me."

We both went up to the counter and ordered our food, then came back to sit down. There is something mouthwatering about the smell of beef cooking. Damn. I was distracted as we sat back down to wait for the food. I kept the chit chat light.

"So how do you like working for Jonathan and Ted?"

"It's cool. Jonathan man, he's a trip. Smart, always dresses way cool. You know Ted, he's a good guy, just kinda uptight."

"You like the work?"

"I love it. It's all cutting edge research."

"Where'd you go to school?"

"Stanford."

"That's impressive."

"Ted went there, but then you probably already know that. Anyway, he keeps close ties with Stanford. He wrote a letter of recommendation for me to get in."

"How does he know your family?"

"My father is an engineer. Ted has visited China a fair amount, working with some researchers from the China National Space Administration. You know China's space program is something they are really pumping a lot of research into."

"I've heard that. So, Ted and your father are friends?"

"Professionally, that's about it. But he had dinner at our house numerous times when I was a teenager. We hit it off and when he found out I was interested in going to Stanford he wrote a letter of recommendation for me."

"Your English is good."

"Better than most American's speak it."

I laughed. "Very true."

"So you just stayed here in this country after you graduated."

"Yeah, Ted kept up with me at Stanford. When I got my masters he asked me if I wanted a job doing research."

"Does everybody there get along pretty well?"

"Oh yeah, we're tight. Nancy, Rupert and me are tight. Nancy is quiet, keeps to herself a lot. Rupert is a wild man. He and I party."

"Does Jonathan come to the lab much?"

"A few times a week."

"How does everybody get along with Jonathan?"

"I don't know. He's an arrogant prick, but man he always has some hot chick on his arm or is driving a hot car. I mean, he's got it goin' on."

A person from behind the counter brought out our food. It smelled so damn good. My burger was incredible. I ordered blue cheese on it along with some other unique toppings you don't see at most places. They even offer foie gras. But, since the blue cheese would have obliterated the taste of it, I just went for the cheese.

We sat down and dug in. I was ravenous. For about two minutes all we did was eat. I paced myself so I could savor the food. The fries were very good with it. As my hunger pangs abated I looked over at Reggie. His burger was gone and half of his fries as well.

"How was your burger?" I asked.

"Good. It's always good here."

He studied me a moment and took another sip of beer.

"Well, how can I help you?"

"Do you know what's going on Reggie?"

"Yeah, Ted told us all yesterday."

"What did he tell you?"

"That we are victims of corporate theft. He said a bunch of our research was taken."

"Do you think anyone in your office might be involved in this in any way?"

"Stealing from Jon-Jon and Ted? Nah, Nancy is too timid and Rupert man, the only shit he cares about outside of work is partying and gaming."

"Maybe Nancy's timidity is an act."

Reggie laughed. "You obviously have never met her. She's cool and smart, but she jumps ten feet in the air if a leaf falls out of a tree next to her."

"What about Rupert? Maybe selling the secrets of your company will keep him in coke or smack for a long time."

"Listen Frank, Rupert doesn't give a shit about anything outside of his geeky ass hobbies and getting high."

"Is he smart?"

"Super smart."

I paused and took another bite of my burger. "Have you ever taken anything from SPURRIER AND FREEN Reggie?"

"Some ballpoint pens, some blank cd's."

"Nothing bigger?"

He narrowed his eyes at me.

"Could you please answer the question?" I said in a neutral tone of voice.

"Look dude, we periodically have to go through lie detector tests as part of the regular security measures. Even in an office our size we have to leave our purses and backpacks in a locker when we first report to work."

"You didn't answer the question." I took another bite of the burger and got a big chunk of blue cheese in it.

"No man. Ted has helped me out a lot. I would never do shit like that to him man. He's a good guy. I owe him. And my father would feel disgraced if I did that to Ted. Honor is a big thing with my father."

"Have you ever noticed anyone else take

things home from the office that they weren't supposed to? Or have you ever suspected any of them of sneaking copies of things out of the office?"

"No." He was now completely on the defensive.

"Reggie, this is nothing personal. Ted likes you a lot and doesn't suspect you of anything. I am being paid to get to the bottom of what happened. I need to ask questions."

He just sat and stared at me.

"Have you ever had anyone approach you and ask any unusual questions about the company or ask you to get any information for them?"

"Of course."

"Who?"

"Look, we interact with other researchers from some other labs and the military. We share some info. They do too. I do the same thing with them."

"But are there any that seem to push it more or ever ask you to get information for them, to pay you for it?"

"No."

I watched him as I took another bite, chewed it slowly, took a large quaff of beer and let it linger in my mouth a long minute. He sat staring back at me. He was a prideful little shit.

"We done?" He asked.

"Yeah."

He got up, went to the counter and paid his tab. He turned toward me as he left and said, "Later dude."

I sat and quietly finished my meal. I have to say the burger was damn good. They clearly used good blue cheese that had a real bite to it.

As I was finishing my fries I called Ted. I got the name of Reggie's father and then called Dogbone and asked him to gather everything he could about him.

Chapter 18

I headed back across the river. At 2:00 I
had a meeting with the CEO from Future Tech
Engineering. Like many companies, they had a
downtown office where they could hobnob and
rub elbows with people on Capitol Hill and the
Pentagon. Ted had called their office and asked
for an appointment. Their downtown office was
on the second floor of an old brownstone walk
up near 22nd and K Street. It was only ten
block's from Fiona's so I parked my car and
walked over.

Their office was posh. Overstuffed
leather chairs and couches, expensive
reproductions of Monet's hanging on the wall
and several large tropical plants in ceramic
planters gave an overall air of class. A nicely

dressed, middle-aged secretary took my name when I arrived. She wore tortoiseshell glasses and had her hair pulled back into an old fashioned bun like an old schoolmarm.

"Mr. Petrucelli will see you in a few moments," she stated very matter-of-factly.

I sat down and was swallowed up by one of the overstuffed chairs. They had various tech magazines on the coffee table along with recent issues of Psychology Today. I went for the latter. Petrucelli kept me waiting for thirty minutes. I asked the schoolmarm if he was in a meeting. She said he wasn't, just very busy.

When I got in to see him the schoolmarm opened his office door and ushered me in. Petrucelli was seated behind his desk. He stood up and motioned with his hand for me to come in.

His office was as posh as the reception area. Tall cherry bookcases loaded with numerous sets of books, many looking like technical journals. His desk was mahogany, and covered in files and loose papers. A large scientific calculator sat beside a legal pad in the middle. His chair was tall backed and looked like something a judge in a courtroom sits in. The carpet was a large Persian rug, royal blue with intricate little designs. The wall to the right of his desk was adorned in framed certificates, and in the dead center of it all behind glass was one that with a cursory glance I picked up the words Yale and PhD.

"Come in, come in Mr., uh…….."

"Frank Goulet," I stated as I moved toward him with my hand extended. We clasped hands and I looked him in the eyes. He looked right back, full of confidence and strength.

"Robert Petrucelli," he announced with verve.

He had white hair, neatly cropped. He couldn't have been more than fifty. He dressed impeccably, with a pink shirt and expensive blue tie. His sleeves were rolled up. He had unnaturally piecing blue eyes which I could only assume were from colored contacts. He motioned me to have a seat with a wave of his hand.

"Would you like some coffee?"

"No thank you Mr. Petrucelli." I sat down and shifted in my chair to get comfortable as he settled in across his desk from me.

Petrucelli leaned back in his chair, looking more like a judge now eyeing the complainant before him. "Ted asked me to see you. He said they had some type of a break in at SPURRIER AND FREEN."

"That's right. I am a former DC Detective and now private investigator. They would like to keep the police out of it initially until we know what happened."

Petrucelli's mouth rose on one side into a

sardonic smile. "So, what exactly has Ted lost?"

"Some documents were stolen regarding research they are doing on thermal barrier coatings, ceramics with zirconate something or rathers all for turbofan engines."

Petrucelli smiled warmly with amusement.

"I did a great job butchering that. Did you get the gist of what I was referring to?"

He laughed, "Yes, I'm familiar with their research. So, someone broke in and took some of their research? Interesting."

"Why is that interesting Mr. Petrucelli?"

"I thought Jonathan and Ted ran a very tight ship, followed a lot of protocols. They have a small research team, which should narrow things down a bit."

"Again, why is that interesting?"

He smiled. "Maybe interesting wasn't the best word."

"What would be a better word?"

He lifted his hands, touching his fingertips together forming a steeple and rested his elbows on the arms of his judges chair as he considered me. "How exactly can I help you Mr. Goulet?"

"How familiar are you with the research SPURRIER AND FREEN is doing?"

"Ted and I talk. When you work in the world of aerospace with military applications you know a lot of the main players and you discuss things. We work collaboratively on some projects like this."

"Is the research they are doing on thermal barrier coatings similar in any way to the research and development of your own company?"

"Ceramics have a lot of applications and we have several patents of our own. Regarding ceramics with rare earth zirconates we are in fact working on those, a number of companies are."

"Did you collaborate in any way on research with SPURRIER AND FREEN?"

He stared at me over his fingertips, pursed his lips as if his mind's activity was requiring his face to work along with his synapses. He continued to stare me straight in the eyes without blinking.

"Mr. Goulet, are you wondering if my company stole their research?"

"Yes, I am."

He chuckled. "I might have been interested in their research a year and a half or two years ago, but not now."

"Why is that?"

"Stella Buccino. She was the brainchild of the research they are doing, or perhaps I should say, were doing. No, when Jonathan fired her the research stopped almost dead in the water."

"How do you know so much about their research?"

"I've seen the proposals with test results

they've sent to the military. I've met with the same people they have to make my own proposals. I know from talking to Aberdeen Proving Grounds that SPURRIER AND FREEN is not where they need to be with their research or development. You get to know people in the field and they talk off the record. I've heard things."

"Well sir, if you don't mind me asking, why then do you think someone would steal their research?"

Petrucelli leaned back in his chair and put his hands behind his head. "They have some great ideas and some great research, it's just that when Stella left I believe it didn't go much further. They have a few young firecrackers on the research now, but no one with a lot of deep knowledge. So, if someone had a chance to steal it so they could build on it, maybe that's why. I mean, from what I understand their concept is excellent, they just haven't been able to move it to the next level."

"So who might be interested?"

"Oh hell, maybe the Chinese, they could use it in their space program as well. Maybe Russia or several R&D companies in the U.S. I mean, if it was available to take, maybe they would risk it."

"You sound doubtful someone would risk stealing it."

"I would be interested to see it, but would

I risk corporate theft for research that has gone nowhere in a year and a half? No. My own company has a different concept that is much closer to fruition."

I thanked him for his time and headed home.

Chapter 19

Angel picked me up in his white Ford Econovan at 4:30. It was unmarked with no windows in the back section. He had it loaded down with enough firepower to arm a small third world nation.

I slid up into the passenger side.

"How you doin' boss man?" Angel asked.

"Vexed."

"Hm," Angel grunted, steering clear of my comment. He changed the subject. "So, what's the scenario for tonight?"

"I'll go check into my room at The Modicum and they will meet me in the room. I'm supposed to call him and tell him the room number once I check in. You hang outside and keep an eye out for the red Cadillac and see if the lady shows up." I handed him a photo of Petra which I printed from their website. "Then you follow the Caddie. I spoke to Tina today down in Vice. She knows this guy Dex, says he's a badass and likely has made several girls vanish. So be careful with him."

Angel smiled.

"Seriously, just watch your ass and do what you do best."

"You want me to kill him?"

"No dickhead, extract information from him, interrogate him."

"Oh, well, just for the record, killing him would be what I do best."

"Yeah, I got that. You're biceps must have been blocking your ears. Sorry for confusing you with details."

"So while I'm pulling his finger nails and applying electricity to his private parts what are you going to be doing, getting laid by the hooker? You might as well, Spurrier is picking up the bill."

"God Angel, are you really so low class?"

"Hey, I shoot people for a living, so excuse me if I don't hold my teacup with my little pinky sticking out."

"Well, to answer you idiotic question, I am going to be trying to extract any information I can from her related to Charlotte and see if she has dealt with Jonathan before."

"Oh, well, I guess that's why you're a

detective and I just pull the trigger. See, I would've just gone up there and had a good time since it's on the clients tab."

I shook my head. Sometimes Angel mystifies me.

"By the way, I spoke with Dogbone earlier but I forgot to ask him for an update. You know where he is with setting up surveillance?" I asked.

"Yeah, I spoke with him an hour ago. He's using a bunch of spyware apps that are all technically legal. They are the kind of crap parents buy to spy on their kid's cell phones so they can read their e-mails and track where they are."

"It's all legit?"

"He says the apps are perfectly legal to purchase and for parents to use because they own their kids phones. They aren't legal for us to install on someone else's phones, but, Dogbone says he can install them by imbedding the app into their phone through their voicemail. Once he's in their phone he can download their whole contact list, all of their text messages, whatever banking info and e-mailing they do over the phone."

"Shit, that's scary."

"Tell me about it."

"Hm, well, this should be interesting."

As we chatted Angel was trying like hell to negotiate Washington afternoon traffic.

Traffic sucked. People were bottlenecked with cross streets running red lights and then getting stuck out in the middle of intersections with nowhere to go when the lights changed. As Angel mumbled to himself and cut a few people off I reached around behind me and pulled out my Sig Sauer 9 millimeter, pulled the slide back and looked into the chamber. I always double check if there's one in the chamber, no matter how many times I've already done it.

Angel glanced over as I went through my little ritual. "You want something with a little more poop?"

"Nope, I'm good with my Sig."

"Man, alright, but if you wanna upgrade I've got some Glocks in .40 cal, uh, and I've got a good ole .45 Colt Commander."

"I'm good my man. I can squeeze off two in rapid succession with my Sig and put 'em both in the same hole."

"Alright. Well, here let me give you this." Angel reached down onto the floor and picked up a small box. He handed it to me. Inside was a small ear piece and a microphone. I took them both out and looked them over.

"Is it already turned on?"

"It's good to go, just stick it in your ear."

I took the small device out of the box and gently pushed it into my ear, then clipped the mike inside my collar.

"You got it in?" Angel asked.

"Yeah, test it."

"Okay." Angel tilted his chin down toward the collar on his jacket where he always keeps his microphone. "Testing, one, two, three."

"Yeah, I can hear it loud and clear." We drove on in silence as Angel headed down K Street, then turned right on 16th Street and made our way over to The Modicum. The hotel was in a nice section of town, probably like a three or three and a half star hotel. He dropped me off three blocks away in case Dex was around and might see me getting out of the van. I walked to The Modicum, went inside and checked in. Once I was in my room I called Dexter Deahl and told him what room I was in. He said his lady would see me at 8:30.

I had four hours to kill so I ventured out of the hotel and headed over to a very nice Belgian restaurant called The Brugges where I could get great authentic Belgian food. I got a fabulous Carbonnade and a Grimbergen Blonde and fries to go with it. There is nothing like piping hot Belgian fries and a Belgian beer on a chilly day. I kept the receipt and figured I would charge that to Jonathan's tab as well, after all, I was only here while I was waiting on Dex.

Chapter 20

I was lounging on the bed in the hotel, surfing through the channels of movies On Demand when I heard Angel's voice crackling in my ear. "Hey boss man, I think your little friends are here to play."

"You got the red caddie?"

"I do. And I see the lady you gave me the photo of."

"Is he coming in with her?"

"No, she is heading inside and he is pulling away from the curb."

"Alright, you find a nice spot to talk to him. If he is uncooperative then snatch his ass and be a little more persuasive. I will work my end of things up here."

"I'm on it. And just for the record, the

hooker who's coming up is quite a hottie, prettier in person than her photo. You might want to tap that just for the fun of it before you get her out of the mood with all of your detective bullshit."

"You go play with the pimp and leave the thinking side of things to the detectives."

"Right Sherlock."

It was about five minutes before I heard the ding of the elevator on my floor. The hallway was carpeted so I heard nothing else until there was a knock on the door. I opened the door to see a very nice looking blonde wearing a low cut blue tank top that could barely contain her two large attributes it was wrestling to hold in place. She was about five foot four, blue eyes and a big smile. Her facial features were somewhat plain with a large nose, yet her eyes and smile made her very attractive. She appeared to be in her mid-twenties, and was wearing a tiny black mini skirt that clung to her like Saran wrap.

"Hi, I'm Petra."

"Wow, god, you're even prettier in person than on the website."

She smiled. "Are you Harry Stenser?"

"Yes I am."

"Good, well, can I come in?"

"Where are my manners? Of course, come in." I stepped aside and opened the door to let her pass.

She walked in and looked around, scoping out the room. I got the impression she was looking to make sure there weren't any surprises waiting for her, smart woman. Once she was satisfied she turned around and set her purse on the bed. When she turned to look at me I have to admit, she had a body that made it very difficult to think straight.

She stared at me with her big blue eyes. They were sweet eyes but had a faraway look in them. She was friendly and cute in her own way.

"Before we get started I need to ask you, are you a police officer?" She asked.

"No, I'm not."

She smiled. "Sorry, but I have to check."

"I understand."

She sat down on the bed, her mini skirt no longer hiding anything that was underneath. She leaned back onto one arm and her smile became more coquettish. "Why don't you have a seat Mr. Harry Stenser?"

Ooh boy, it was a damn good thing I didn't let Angel handle this side of the investigation. This lady could have brought any man to their knees. Sometimes I think that if women actually knew how much power they have over men they would simply take over the world and put all of us drooling dogs into a kennel somewhere where they could just put leashes on us and take us out anytime they simply wanted to entertain themselves.

I stepped over to the bed and sat down beside her.

"You have me for as long as you need me," she said, tilting her chin down slightly as she spoke. Her eyes were soft and seductive. She reached over with her hand and gently laid it on the inside of my thigh. God she knew her craft well. It was difficult to concentrate.

"Petra, can we talk for a few minutes?"

"You nervous? Have you never been with an escort before?"

I smiled. She smiled back and furrowed her brow, looking puzzled.

"Look, you are," I paused and laughed. I adjusted my sitting angle, turning more to face her dead on. "You are gorgeous. And I am going to pay you for your time, but the truth is I need to talk to you."

She looked surprised and chuckled slightly. "Are you nervous about cheating on your wife or something?"

"No, that's not the issue here. I need to ask you about Charlotte."

Her face looked suspicious. She stood up.

"You are a cop."

"No, no, I'm not. Charlotte took something from a client of mine. I need to get it back."

"Who are you?"

"I'm a private detective and if you can

help me find it I will not only pay you what I owe you tonight but I will give you an extra five thousand dollars."

Her eyes lit up. "Are you for real?"

"100%. You help me out and I will give you whatever I owe you plus five grand." As I said it I reached into back pocket, pulled out my wallet and took out one of my cards. I handed it to her. She took it and stared at it a long moment.

"Frank Goulet? You're not Harry Stenser?"

"I'm the person on the card, a private detective."

She relaxed and smiled again. She really was very pretty when she smiled. "Huh, I never met a private eye before."

"I work for a man who says he has been with Charlotte many times right here at this hotel. His name's Jonathan Spurrier."

Her eyes grew wide, clearly indicating she recognized the name, but she didn't smile.

"You know him?"

She sat down on the bed staring at my card as she answered. "I know him."

"Has he been a client of yours?"

"He beat the shit out of me one night. He tied me to a bed and knocked one of my teeth loose. I had two black eyes and couldn't work for a week. He, well, let's just say he rode me really, really hard that night, over and over again. I asked him to stop. He just laughed. He seemed to get turned on the more I asked him to stop. He's a sick asshole."

She suddenly looked small and fragile. Her stare looked far away and there was pain in her eyes.

"Didn't Dex do anything to Jonathan for doing that?"

"Are you crazy? Jonathan just pays extra when he hurts us. Dex makes more money."

"I uh, I don't know what to say."

She looked at me, studying my face. I had seen that look before when I worked the streets. She had learned to hide pain somewhere deep down inside, but it was still there, beneath the surface.

"I'm sorry. I really am."

She looked into my eyes, studying me for a long moment. "Why are you working for him?"

"It's a favor for a friend of mine. And just for the record, I hate the son of a bitch."

She smiled.

"Look, Charlotte took his briefcase. I need to get it back."

"Are you sure Charlotte took it?"

"According to Jonathan she did. And the clerks at the desk downstairs corroborated that."

"I can't imagine Charlotte doing that. Dex would beat the living shit out of her if she stole from one of the clients. Or, he might do something worse."

"You're saying you don't think Charlotte would cross Dex by stealing?"

"I don't think there's any way she would. Charlotte lived with me for a few months. I let her stay in my apartment. Believe me, she's not dumb enough to steal from Dex or Xavier. The last girl I know who stole anything from them disappeared. We all know what happened. Believe me, Charlotte wouldn't take it."

"Do you think Dex might have asked her to do it?"

She stopped and thought about that. "I've never heard of him doing it. We deal with a lot of rich clients. He makes more by staying honest with them than by stealing from them. And he tells all the girls when they first start working for him that they better never lift anything off a client."

"Interesting," I stated, trying to digest how this fit in with what happened.

"Plus, I don't think he's dumb enough to cross Xavier."

"Let me ask you something, how smart would you say Dex is?"

"How smart?"

"Yeah, I mean is he clever, good with numbers or money or flimflamming people?"

"Oh, he's smart. He hustles people for a living, knows how to intimidate people and how to sucker them out of money. He's very smart."

"Makes sense, he's a hustler. Let's talk about Jonathan for a second. Did Charlotte ever talk about him? It sounds like she saw him a lot."

"All the time. She liked him a lot. She didn't mind him beating the shit out of her. He paid her a lot. She was kinda twisted in her own way. I think she was kinda into the whole S&M thing. Some girls are. God, sometimes she would come back to the apartment with bruises all over her."

"She said she liked him a lot?"

"I think she loved him. I think she somehow thought he was her Richard Gere."

I involuntarily pulled my head back and looked at her questioningly. "What are you talking about?"

"You know Richard Gere? Like in the movie Pretty Woman, when the rich man falls in love with the prostitute and takes her away from all of that?"

I started laughing. "God, the hooker version of Cinderella."

"I know," Petra said. "Charlotte's only about seventeen, still believes her fairy godmother is going to rescue her from her evil stepmother."

There was a long pause. Then Petra added, "Plus, I know Charlotte and Jonathan's wife have a thing."

"What?"

"Oh yeah, Jonathan had three ways with Charlotte and his wife and Charlotte said it seemed like his wife was really into her."

"Really into her as in not just into the three ways, but really has a thing for Charlotte?"

"That's what Charlotte said."

Damn, that one totally blindsided me. Petra had grown quiet. I studied her as she sat quietly staring down at my card. She was smart and savvy.

After a long moment she said, "Do you think Charlotte is okay?"

"You probably know better than I do. Do you think she's okay?"

She tilted her head down and didn't answer. I instinctively reached over and brushed her hair back behind her ear and said, "Do you mind if I ask you a personal question?" She looked up.

"Why do you do this? You're gorgeous, you're smart, you seem......."

"Too good to be doing something like this?" She said, cutting me off.

"I guess so."

She stared down at her hands. "I have two kids, a daughter and a son. I was an internet bride from Albania. After having two kids my American husband lost interest and bolted. I was out on the street with two kids and no money. I was twenty two. It's hard finding work, especially when you have two kids at home, a green card and no skills. We were going to be evicted from our apartment. I met a guy. He told me I could make money dancing at a club. Then Dex came in." She looked up at me. "I'd do anything for my kids, anything." She shrugged her shoulders. "Now I can afford to have them in day care, we have a television and they eat good."

"Do you regret doing it?"

"I'm a whore Frank. I screw nasty dirty old men and young horny guys who hire me for parties. I entertain pudgy politicians and visiting diplomats. But I have kids to feed. It doesn't matter if I regret it."

"Hey, at least you're way of screwing people is more honest than the way the politicians screw them."

She smiled slightly in spite of herself. She glanced over at me with slightly playful eyes. "It's too bad you really weren't my client tonight. Maybe for once I would have had a guy who was at least a little more fun to be with."

"A little? Hell, I would have had you rolling on the floor in stitches. Did I tell you my other job is doing standup at the Comedy Club?"

"Well, you surely would go broke in that line of work, so I guess it's good you're a private eye."

It was my turn to smile at her. "Touché."

She relaxed and laid back on the bed, putting her arms behind her head. She looked up at me, "Look, I don't know what else I can tell you about Charlotte. I heard she bolted. I didn't know why. I still find it hard to believe that she took Jonathan's briefcase, but who knows? She told me that he was going to take her away from all of this, set her up somewhere as his private concubine or mistress or whatever."

She was very pretty just lying there on the bed. She looked so relaxed that it seemed more like we were just old friends having a chat.

"Any ideas where she might have bolted to?"

"She might have headed up to New York or down south to Miami and gone over to another service down there. There's a lot of money to be made in New York or Miami. Everybody liked Charlotte. She's gorgeous and cute and will pretty much do anything a client wants."

"Did she ever leave any kind of home address or the name of some person she stays in touch with?"

"No, she was very private. I know she ran away from home because her mother and father were brutal to her. She hated them. I think she was just happy to be gone from her old life."

There was a pause. I studied her a long moment. It was then I noticed the bruises on her thighs and five small bruises on her left bicep that was clearly from someone grabbing her hard in a tight grip. She noticed me staring, sat up and lowered her arm to hide it.

"That from Dex?"

She turned red. "He got a little pissed the other night. It was my fault."

I didn't know what to say so I kept my mouth shut. There was a long moment of awkward silence. I studied her as she stared down at the floor. I thought about her kids. She regained her composure and looked up with those big blue eyes and smiled. "I like you Frank."

I smiled back at her.

"Look," she said in a huskier tone. "You're paying me to be here anyway. I like you. You're one of the nicest guys I've been with. Do you want to have sex anyway? You are paying for it."

She said it so matter-of-factly. I sat there beside her and stared down into her eyes. I could see that it was no big deal to her. It was a completely passionless procedure, very matter of fact. It was her job and she was used to making men happy for a living.

"You are beautiful Petra, but somehow it would just seem like a business transaction. It kinda takes the luster out of it."

"Oh, I can put luster into it," she said, her eyes taking on a deeply alluring quality.

I shook my head, smiled and said, "Petra,

you are far more dangerous than any drug dealer or murderer I ever locked up or shot."

"Why is that?"

"Because I knew exactly how to deal with them me. But you, you are too damn beautiful and you are a sweetheart. Something tells me you can make men do pretty much whatever you want."

"Men are pretty easy to control."

"You've got that right," I said with a laugh.

"Well if you like me Frank you could be my sugar daddy."

"Ha, something tells me you already have a few of those."

She smiled again. "I do. They're regulars and they tip me well. If only the other mothers at my kid's preschool knew that it was their husbands who are paying for my kids to play with theirs."

I burst out laughing. She started laughing too. After a long moment I looked at her again.

"You know Petra, I like you too." I leaned over and gently kissed her forehead. "I genuinely like you. And believe me, I don't like many people."

She smiled. "Thank you Frank. You're alright."

It was then I heard the crackle of Angel's voice in my ear. "I got him boss. Do you copy? I got ole Mr. Dexter for you."

I tilted my lips down toward my collar. "Did you try to talk to him?"

Petra stared at me with a puzzled look.

"I'm talking to my partner," I said.

"Hm," she mumbled.

"Yeah, I talked to him alright. The third time he told me to go fuck myself he pulled a knife on me, and let's just say he ain't gonna be using that hand for a while. Then I duct taped his ass and threw him in the back of the van."

"Alright, where are you?"

"Two blocks east of your location in an alley on the south side of the street."

"Ten four, I'll see you in a few minutes."

I turned to Petra. She was staring up at me. I took out my wallet again and handed her a giant wad of cash, generously compensating her for her time.

"Listen Petra, you have my card. If you hear anything else or think of anything else call me and let me know. I'll pay you for any additional information you find."

"Okay, I'll see what I can find out."

"Hey listen, if you ever want to get out of this line of work there is a woman named Dani who I do a lot of work for. She's a good friend and she owes me a huge favor. She would actually really like you. She's tough, smart and savvy. She's looking for an assistant right now who can deal with her clients, schedule them, set up big fancy parties and soirees."

"Thanks Frank, but I don't really think I would fit in that world of big rich people. Plus, I've probably been hired to sleep with some of her clients before."

"Ha, let me tell you Miss Petra, half those people have slept with each other's wives or mistresses or their secretaries. No, you would probably be one of the most honest ones among them."

She laughed again. "Thanks Frank. I'll think about it."

I stood up and turned to face her. "Look, I gotta go. But, while you're here you might as well order room service and help yourself to the minibar. It's all being paid for by Jonathan anyway, so at least you can feel like you're getting a little bit of sweet revenge."

She stood up and pulled her mini skirt down and smoothed it out. "I really should probably just go. I can get home in time to see the kids before they go to bed."

We exited the room together and rode the elevator down. Outside on the street we paused and I turned to face her.

"You know what? I really enjoyed meeting you Petra."

She furrowed her brow and looked at me with a slightly bewildered look. "You are not like other men Frank, you know that?"

"I know, damn it. That's why I can never get laid."

"Hey, I offered," she countered playfully.

"I know, what kind of man turns down someone as gorgeous as you?"

"A really nice guy."

"Now don't get mushy or you're going to make me blush."

I stepped forward and gave her a big hug. She put her arms around my waist and hugged me back.

"You take care of yourself Petra. And if you ever need anything, or are in trouble, you give me a call. You can also always leave a message at Fiona's. It's a bar on M Street in Georgetown. I live above the bar and Fiona and I are good friends. She will know where to find me."

"You really are a sweet man Frank."

"That's always been my biggest problem."

I released her from our hug. She looked up at me, slightly misty eyed as we parted.

Chapter 21

When I got to the van Angel was sitting in the front seat reading a Guns and Ammo Magazine. I climbed into the passenger side. I heard Dex stir in the back as I climbed in.

"How'd it go?" Angel asked.

"She's a good kid, but had no answers for us." I lied because Dex could overhear my reply.

"Did you tap it?"

"God Angel you mystify me sometimes. I'll bet if you ever do that genetic research thing to look at your ancestral line they are going to declare that you didn't simply descend from Australopithecus, but in fact you will prove that Australopithecus never died out."

"What the fuck are you talking about?"

"Never mind, tell me about our man

Dexter here."

Angel glanced over his shoulder at Dex. "Oh, he's a tough guy. Pulled a knife on me."

"Yeah, you mentioned that."

Angel smiled as he stared at Dex. "Yeah, a fucking little stilletto."

"I didn't know people still carried stillettos."

"Yeah, I think he thinks he's living in the 60's. Anyway, I broke his wrist and I think his nose."

I looked at Dex. I could see blood all over his face and his nose was twisted. "I think it looks good on him."

Dex started mumbling something from beneath the tape over his mouth. He looked furious as he writhed and moved his legs back and forth as if he was trying to get free. Then he winced. I assume tugging on the tape with his broken wrist was the culprit. I turned back to face front. "I'll tell you what, let's get out of here, find some place a little more private."

"You got it boss man." Angel put the van into drive and we pulled out of the alley.

As he negotiated our way out of town I reached into a cooler on the floor and pulled out two ham sandwiches and a block of Gruyere cheese. I rifled through the ice and other things in there and could only find beer.

"You didn't bring any wine?"

"You and your fucking wine. Beer is

good with ham sandwiches."

"Listen Australopithecus, beer is good, but you don't fucking drink beer with Gruyere cheese. Goddamn, how dense are you son?"

"You goddamn French people are such a pain in the ass."

"Hey, ape man, do you have any taste buds at all?"

I handed him his sandwich and popped the top of a beer for him. "You brought fucking PBR's?"

"I like Pabst. Plus they're only $4.99 for a six pack."

I just shook my head and handed him his beer. I took out my pocket knife and cut off some slices of Gruyere cheese and offered him one.

"No thanks, I'll just go for the ham and beer."

We drove on. We crossed the Potomac River and turned onto the George Washington Parkway heading north. Traffic really moved now and if it weren't for the fact that we had a kidnapped, duct taped, beat up pimp in the back of the van, it would have been a gorgeous scenic drive as the road lifted up high above the Potomac and had a panoramic view out over Washington.

As we cruised up the parkway I looked through the personal items Angel had taken off Dex when he frisked him. His stiletto, wallet, keys, cell phone and about a dozen Trojan condoms of various sizes. I went through his wallet. It was a typical guy wallet, stuffed with money, credit cards and a million little notes and receipts. There was a folded up check someone had written to him over a month ago which he hadn't even cashed for $324. I took all the notes and receipts and put them in an envelope. Then I took his cell phone and called Dogbone.

"Bone's pizza delivery, how may I help you?"

I laughed. "You are such a geek."

There was a pause. I knew Dogbone wouldn't recognize the phone I was calling from. But, as always, he surprised me. "Hey Frank-furter."

"You are frightening. How the hell did you know it was me?"

"I already downloaded everything off of Jonathan's phone, got all his phone numbers, texts, whatever. Plus, I've been tracking you guys, so the little blips of your van and this incoming telephone match, so, there you go."

"Goddamn you are scary."

I spoke softly now so Dex couldn't hear. "I want you to download all info off of this phone, phone numbers, texts, any online banking transactions. Go through any history of websites that look notable."

"Gotcha Frankie. And when you hang up I will delete this outgoing call from his phone so that there's no record of me and I remain the invisible man."

I signed off with Dogbone. Then I quickly perused his contact list - Xavier, Jonathan, Petra, and bingo, Charlotte. For reference I jotted down people's numbers.

By the time I put the phone down we had reached the end of the parkway and were exiting onto the Beltway, where we got on and headed back across the river into Maryland and got off at the exit for Carderock on MacArthur Boulevard. Suddenly we were surrounded by thick forests as the road began paralleling the C&O Canal. We passed the brightly lit compound of the Naval Research Lab and plunged into almost complete darkness as the forest suddenly engulfed us and we continued north. After several more minutes we turned off onto a tiny service road. I got out with some bolt cutters and cut the chain that went across it. We continued up the road, deep into the woods. When Angel finally pulled over I stuffed the last bite of my second sandwich into my mouth and swung my legs around so I could look into the back of the van.

Keep in mind that when you want to interrogate a hard ass, you first need to establish who the alpha dog in the relationship is. First you need to show them your muscles, rough 'em up a little to get their attention and so they know you are aren't dicking around. Then leave them in isolation for a bit for their imagination to start kicking in and for it dawn on them that their little tough guy act won't buy them jack shit off the streets. Then, like any good steak, after letting it marinate a bit to tenderize it, you just add some butter, olive oil and whatever you were marinating it in and it will almost cook itself. The real work is in the preparation.

I hunched over as I walked back to where Dex was laying. I opened the van door so he could see it was completely pitch black outside and we were deep in a forest. I looked at his face. He looked terrified. I pulled out an ASP collapsible steel baton and flipped it open. It ratcheted out with a loud metallic snap. Dex flinched.

I knelt down beside him and spoke in a quiet voice. "Dex, I am going to remove the tape from your mouth. If you scream I will break your legs. Do we understand each other?"

He nodded.

I reached down and ripped the tape from across his mouth. I could hear some skin tear and he screamed in pain. The ASP flashed through the air like a lightning bolt and smashed into his shins. He started to scream but then changed it to a loud muffled groan. He writhed back and forth on the floor of the van, moaning and biting his lip to keep from screaming.

"Dex, why are you making me do this? My friend here tells me he asked you some simple questions and you pulled a knife on him. That was really not very nice Dex."

"Hm, hm," he groaned, writhing from the pain in his shins.

"Okay, now, I am going to ask you a few questions. You really need to consider how tough you want to make this. You know Angel and I have a whole cooler full of beer, a bunch of sandwiches and no place in particular to be. And even though it is only Pabst Blue Ribbon," I turned and looked at Angel, "which is actually pretty good, just not with Gruyere cheese, we could be here for a really long time."

I paused to let that sink in.

"Now, what do you know about the disappearance of Jonathan Spurrier's briefcase?" He looked at me nervously. He spoke quietly, looking back and forth between Angel and me. "I swear, I don't know nothin'. That little bitch Charlotte just bolted after she left Jonathan."

I stared at him a long moment.

"I swear. I swear. It's the truth."

I lifted the ASP up. He flinched. I rested it gently on my shoulder.

"Let's say I believe you. Why in the world would Charlotte do that? My friends down in Vice Squad tell me that whenever your girls steal or do anything that you don't like you either beat the shit out of them or they just disappear."

He looked terrified again.

"Do you like beating the shit out of ladies Dexter? Does that give you some kind of a thrill?"

He wisely didn't answer but just kept staring at me like a terrified little creature.

"Did you make Charlotte disappear Dex?"

"No, no, fuck no. Jonathan has a real thing for her. He pays me shit loads of money for her. I wouldn't do that. It would be bad business."

"Hm, you are a business man aren't you Dex? Even your name, Dexter Deahl, what a great name for a guy who sells women on the street."

He didn't say anything.

"I'll tell you what Dexter Deahl, I'm going to make a DEAL with you. You better give me something I need to know or your ass is going to be floating in the C&O Canal."

"I, I swear, I don't know shit."

I thought of Petra. I thought of the bruises on her arm and thighs and how this bastard let Jonathan beat the shit out of her. The ASP flashed through the air and he screamed and then closed his mouth and groaned and winced and made little pathetic sounds.

"So, you like beating up your girls huh?" The ASP flashed again. He screamed like an animal. "Do you like that Dex? Huh, do you like how that feels? I wonder how your girls like it."

All I could think about was Petra. I raised the ASP again and Angel caught my wrist. "Hey boss man, I don't want to interfere with your fun, but uh, you know………"

I turned and looked at him. My arm relaxed. I looked down at Dex. "You're a lucky man Dex. My friend here is a softy."

Dex stared at Angel and then at me.

"Alright Dex, I'm tired of being nice about this. You tell me something I need to know. And it better goddamn well be something useful. You answer yes or no to the following questions. First, did you hurt Charlotte, or do you know where she is?"

"No, no, I didn't touch her and I don't know where she is."

I studied his face. He was a street rat and a hustler. He was damn good at lying. It's what he did for a living. And he was good at hiding it.

"Did you have Charlotte take the briefcase?"

"No."

I raised the ASP.

"No, no, fuck no, I didn't have her take the goddamn briefcase!" He shouted.

"Did you take it?"

"No."

The ASP flashed through the air. He screamed. "Ahhhhhhhhhhhhhhhh."

"Did you take it Dex?"

"No goddamn it. I didn't take the fucking briefcase!" He rolled back and forth, grimacing with his eyes squeezed tightly shut as he dealt with the pain.

I watched him for a long moment. He partially opened his eyes. There was a rodent like quality to them, the eyes of a survivor who will do whatever it takes. He came from the streets and that's the way it is. But, even though it was hard to separate which things he was lying about I knew he would be useful to me anyway.

"How can I believe you Dex, huh?"

"Are you fucking crazy? After what you guys just did to me? I would be a goddamn idiot to hurt Charlotte now. Look, I'm the one who got screwed in this. I just lost one of my most valuable girls."

I grew quiet and stared down at him, studying him. He got more and more uncomfortable the longer I watched him.

"Look man, I ain't stupid. I wouldn't lie to you. I'm telling you the truth. If she did steal it then she did it on her own. Maybe she was mad at Jonathan. She loved that rich bastard, but maybe she was pissed off at him."

"And how did Jonathan feel about her?"

"He was totally into her. They had a thing going on."

"She's his little Dulcinea, huh?"

"What? Who the hell is Dulcinea? She ain't one of my chicks."

I chuckled. "Oh Dex, the only culture you have is the kind that grows in a little petri dish."

"What?"

"I'll tell you what we're going to do Dexter Deahl." I took one of my cards out of my pocket and I stuffed it into his shirt pocket. "This is my card. You are going to find Charlotte and call me." I leaned in closer now and I stuck the tip of the ASP right up under his nose. "You find her Dex and you don't fucking touch her. You hear me? If she's hurt I will finish what we started tonight. You got that?"

"But……"

I slammed the ASP into the metal wall of the van. The sound was deafening. Dexter curled up into a tight ball and closed his eyes. I spoke softly again. "You got that Dex?"

He simply nodded his head.

We drove in total silence back to D.C. Occasionally I sensed Angel glancing over at me. I didn't look back. Back by the Grand Hotel I cut the duct tape on Dex's wrists and ankles. I opened the van door. Dex stepped out of the van, putting weight on his feet gingerly, wincing slightly as he did from the pain in his shins.

I called out, "Dex?"

He turned slowly, shifting carefully on his feet.

"Dex, for the record, Petra didn't know

anything. I think she was covering up for your sorry ass so I let it slide. I did pay her her fee, so I am square with you on that. I like Petra. In fact, I like her a lot. I will be calling you again in a couple of days to check up on her. If I find out you hurt her in anyway, in any goddamn way at all, I will wax your ass. I will cut your balls off, break your fingers and then wax your ass. If she disappears, you disappear. You got that?"

He just stared at me.

"Dex, do you hear me?"

"I hear you mother fucker." He was starting to get his confidence back now that he was on his own turf.

As we left him standing there I looked back in the side mirror. He was standing very defiantly watching us pull away.

"What the fuck was that about, anyway?" Angel asked.

"I have a feeling he is going to take this out on Petra. He's going to want to know what she told me. He'll interrogate her and beat the hell out of her to find out what she said."

"You think he'll kill her?"

"I don't know." I pulled out my list of phone numbers I had written down from Dex's phone. I called Petra. There was no answer. I figured she was probably already asleep. I left a message for her simply asking her to please call me because I had some important information for her related to Charlotte.

When I disconnected Angel looked over at me. "You okay?"

"Yeah, just concerned."

I was silent a long time.

"Hey Frank, seriously, what has gotten into you? You don't usually give much of a damn for people we go after. Do you like this hooker?"

"You dumb dick, it has nothing to do with that. She's a good woman trying to just get by to save her kids. She gets treated like shit and puts on a good face so she can afford to keep her kids off the street. She's had it tough, gets treated tough, and all she can think about is getting home to tuck her kids in at night. I swear if that son of a bitch touches her they will be fishing pieces of him out of the Anacostia River."

Angel glanced over at me. "She is pretty though, you sure you aren't feeling something for her? You have always been a push over for big pretty eyes and a sad story."

"You know Angel, I saw something in her that hit home. In some ways Petra isn't much different from you or me. It's a hard world and she's a product of it. You and me sell our shady services to the public and see shit most people never see. She does too. We all have kind of sold a little piece of our souls thinking we are doing good for the world, or in her case, for her kids. But the price is high. We're all kind of just damaged goods, you know? We don't really fit in. I feel like the whole damn bunch of us are going to have to be debriefed at the pearly gates when we exit this world, just to make sure we leave all this shitty baggage behind."

Angel had been listening thoughtfully. After a long pause he said, "Well, I sure wouldn't mind letting Petra de-brief me."

I laughed. "I should shoot your ass. You know that?"

"Hey boss, I keep things simple, you know?"

"You big galoot," I said affectionately.

"What the hell is a galoot anyways?"

"It's you my friend."

"You mean someone strong and manly and sophisticated?"

"Yeah, something like that."

He beamed a smile at me. I shook my head and rolled my eyes.

"So Frank, honestly, you didn't, you know? With the hooker?"

"Angel, please. Look, I will admit she is very pretty. And you should see how she works those big blue eyes when she's wearing that miniskirt. You, my friend would not have survived. She would have had you begging her to give it up."

"I ain't gonna lie Frank, it's good you went in there instead of me."

I glanced over at Australopithecus sitting

across from me. "I'll tell you something, Petra has some big sad eyes but if you want to see some really big sad eyes that could melt a man's heart it's Spurrier's wife Lily."

"She pretty?"

"Like a model."

"Damn."

"Alright my gigantic tattooed friend, let's go get a drink."

A big grin spread across his face. "Amen brother."

"Hey, actually, let's go to Fiona's. She's got some punks who are scoping out her place to rob it. Why don't' we go back there and get shit faced."

Fiona was glad to see us. We hung out until closing time but her little robbery suspects didn't show up. But, because we stopped in, drinks were on the house.

Chapter 22

When I woke up in the morning I had a hell of a hangover. I stood under the shower until the hot water ran out, dried off and went downstairs to the pub to eat a good lunch. It was a sunny day. Mitch was already there tossing back a Jack and Coke. It was a Thursday morning. I wondered if this guy really liked being a Jody. He seemed pretty chilled out and happy most of the time. I found myself unconsciously shaking my head back and forth in bewilderment as I stared at him.

I thought it was essential to order a Reuben today. Homicides and tough cases tend to make me crave Reubens washed down with heavy volumes of beer. I suspect it's the age old comfort food craving thing.

Fiona brought my plate out to me.

"Thanks for you and Angel coming by last night," she said.

"Happy to do it. Who knows, maybe the greaser and tubby are scoping out different bars. They may have moved on thinking this one wasn't the best choice."

"Hopefully."

"Well, I may be tied up over the next few nights but I will try to get by around closing time."

"You mean kinky kind of tied up or just tied up with other things?"

"Where the hell is your mind this morning?"

"Where it always is, in a bar," Fiona stated.

"My wild Irish Fiona, I need to take you away from here, take you out dancing one night."

"I thought you didn't dance."

"I don't. That's why I need to take you out, so you can teach me."

She threw her dish towel at me and said, "Eat your damn Reuben." She turned and started to walk back to the kitchen. As she did she cast a glance over her shoulder and said, "By the way, you're late on your rent."

"Oops," I said, more to myself than her, then sunk my teeth into the Reuben.

As I was eating my phone beeped. It was

Petra. "Frank, I was so surprised to see you had called. How did you get my phone number?"

"I'm a detective, what can I say? Listen Petra, I'm sorry to bother you but I was a little worried."

"About what?"

"While I was talking to you last night my partner was asking Dex some questions and let's just say he was not terribly cooperative."

I heard her take in a nervous breath on the other end of the phone.

"You okay?" I asked.

"What happened? Did your partner hurt Dex?"

"Actually, Dex pulled a knife on him. And after my partner knocked him around a bit I went out and joined him and we had a little chat."

There was a long silence. Finally I said, "Petra, I told Dex that you didn't know anything and that I even thought you were covering up for him, so that he would feel like you were loyal to him. I also told him he better not touch you in anyway."

"Did you threaten him?"

"Oh I more than threatened him."

"Why did you do that Frank?"

"Petra......."

"No, no Frank, god, he is going to be crazy as shit now. Oh my god, why did you do that?"

"I did it to protect you Petra."

"No Frank, you don't threaten someone like Dex. Oh my god, you have no idea what he is capable of."

"Hey, I have dealt with a lot of guys on the street Petra. He's not going to touch you. He's not that stupid."

"Oh my god, shit." There was a pause. I could hear her mumbling. "Shit, shit, what the hell am I going to do? Oh my god, he will beat the shit out of me."

"I told him you didn't tell me anything. I tried like hell to cover for you."

"Shit Frank, this is really, really not good." She sounded like she was coming apart. "I uh, I need to think about what to do. I will uh, call you back."

"Petra?"

"Yes Frank?"

"Listen, me and my team can protect you. Why don't you………?"

"Frank, I have to work. I have kids to feed. Shit, listen, I will call you back." She disconnected.

I immediately called Dogbone.

"Yo Frank-furter. Wuz up?"

"I need you to track the phone of one of the hookers off of Dex's contact list. I have a bad feeling that bastard may try to make her disappear. I don't think even he is that stupid, but you never know. Do you have a way to monitor her phone and his and see if they call each other?"

"Of course."

I laughed. "Of course. Okay, well, if either of them calls or texts, record it and let me know ASAP."

"You got it chief."

"Listen, I need you to bring me up to speed on everything. Do you have time to meet today or tonight?"

"Hey, you are the man issuing the paychecks around here, so hey, anything for you."

He was free later in the afternoon so we arranged a meeting at Fiona's.

Chapter 23

I took the rest of the morning off to let my brain try to assimilate things. I headed out Connecticut Avenue to go to the Phillip's Collection, a high class gallery with some of the best exhibits in town. Usually you can take your time there, wander from room to room, sit on the benches and stare at the paintings unmolested by school groups, people pressing tightly against your shoulder, or giggly teenagers.

As I strolled among the exhibits it was the Cezanne's that caught my attention. I was hypnotized by the representational quality, lines and dabs that altogether created the images. One of them on permanent display is a self-portrait. It is such an honest painting, unflattering. It is neither egotistical nor self-deprecating. I always imagine that most people are so egotistical that if they could paint their own self-portraits they would enhance their looks so that every woman would look like Catherine Zeta-Jones and the guys like Pierce Brosnan or Brad Pitt. And I wondered if I could paint, could I do it as honestly as Cezanne?

When I emerged out into the real world again, the day was sunny, chilly and breezy. I walked a block over to Connecticut Avenue. The sycamore trees lining the side streets had the first tiny leaf buds starting to cover the branches. I crossed Connecticut and sat outside a coffee shop on the corner, ordered a cappuccino and watched the world drift by.

This part of Washington is known as Dupont Circle, a colorful mix of the rich, the young, the foreign diplomats, the college students, the gays, the artsy types, the pseudo philosophers, the hip and the bums. I love it. As I sipped my coffee I listened to a pair of twenty something year olds arguing about President Obama and the wars in Afghanistan and Iraq, and the situation in Egypt and Syria and Israel, and if Iran would start World War III. I thought of how these two slugs were probably going to lose their values in another five years as they were absorbed into the typical greed, avarice, narcissism and sloth of the Washington world. Where was the purity of the Cezannes of the world? But then what the hell do I know?

Shit I was restless. The Spurrier case was bugging me. Coming up with hard data was like trying to find a redeeming virtue in Dexter Deahl. It was the nature of the case, reported to me after the fact, a sterilized crime scene, some eyewitnesses and a hell of lot of people who might have good motives to do it. Detective work is so different from when you're a street cop. Street cops deal in more tangible things like stopping a husband from beating his wife, breaking up barroom fights, finding dope while you pat somebody down or giving sobriety tests. Detectives are sorting through bits and pieces and fragments of things to find clues and witnesses. It is very detailed work. You have to be dogged and stubborn as hell sometimes to the point of obsessiveness. But, if you stick to your guns something will turn up. Even the roughest gemstone can be worn down and turned into a gorgeous jewel if you put it in a tumbler and let it stay there long enough. I knew the answers to this case were out there but I didn't yet have that piece that was anchoring everything down and taking me in one direction.

I went home, pounded the shit out of the heavy bag, lifted weights, showered, surfed the web for news of the day and checked my messages.   It was 3:00 when I got a phone call from Dogbone telling me he was downstairs in the bar.

When I pushed through the door into

Fiona's I immediately heard, "Yo Frankie."

I glanced around and saw Dogbone sitting at the bar. He was already working on a Chimay as he sat slump shouldered with a laptop in front of him, wearing his camo BDU pants, and a sleeveless tee shirt with his dark skin and thickly muscled arms hanging out like giant slabs of beef. Dogbone is short and as wide as an oak tree stump. He has the eyes of a falcon that studies everything around him, never missing a goddamn thing. He would look intimidating if it weren't for the perpetually playful puckish grin on his face. The easiest way for me to sum up the difference between Dogbone and Angel is that Angel is a Jack and Coke man while Dogbone loves well-crafted, refined beers, usually Belgian or German. What more can I say?

"Dogbone, long time since I've seen you in the flesh."

"Hey Frankie, sometimes I like to come down and slum around where the white people hang out." He stood up and gave me a big manly hug as I approached.

Fiona was behind the bar washing out glasses in the sink as we sat down. She glanced at us. "Frank, I've been meaning to ask you, what is the deal with Dogbone's nickname?"

I looked at Dogbone and smiled. He just shrugged his shoulders and said, "Go ahead."

"Well, Dogbone and Angel have done a

lot of, well, information gathering over the years for government agencies that don't exist. They were in an undisclosed Middle Eastern country and Dogbone was trying to set up surveillance of a compound where suspected terrorists were meeting. There weren't any kind of structures near the compound within four hundred yards so Dogbone takes a leg bone from an old carcass of a dead dog that is nice and ripe with rotting flesh still on it that has been baking in the sun. He rigs up this great camera. It took him several days to inconspicuously obtain the bone, set it up and get it back into place. Angel says it was a brilliant piece of work."

I glance over at Dogbone and he nods his head and adds, "It's true. It was a beautiful piece of work."

I continued. "Well, damn if on the first day he set it out a mangy old dog didn't come by and carry it off to gnaw on it."

Fiona looked at Dogbone. "Is that true?"

He simply lifted his Chimay up and said, "To all the taxpayer's dollars I have wasted in the name of liberty."

Fiona and I both started laughing.

Fiona looked at me, "What are you having Frank?"

"Do you still have any of that 2007 Marimar Estate Pinot Noir?"

"Yeah, I still have a few bottles."

"Would you mind popping the cork for

your best tenant in the building?"

"Sure, do you want two glasses or one?"

I looked at Dogbone. He lifted his eyebrows and tilted his head slightly to the side as if to say, why not.

He took a pull on his Chimay and said, "Is that a good Pinot Noir?"

"Dogbone, you are in for a treat. Pinot's are finicky grapes that require crazy ass conditions you gotta get just right to make them worth a damn. This is from the Russian River Valley in California where they really know how to grow those grapes. This one from Marimar Estate is elegant, dark and complex."

"Like you my friend," he said as he lifted his beer toward me.

"Haha, yeah, like me."

Fiona brought out the bottle already uncorked and set it on the bar. As I poured us each a glass Dogbone tilted his Chimay up and finished it. I slid a glass of the Pinot over to him. We touched glasses, took a sip and then he directed my attention to his computer screen.

"Alright Frankie, here's what we've got. I was able to break into Jonathan's phone right off. From that I made my way into his wife's phone, Ted's, and the uh, whatever the little Asian dude's name is……"

"Reggie Tsui," I interjected.

"Yeah, the Chinaman, anyway, the list goes on and on as you can see."

I looked at his computer screen. He had each person broken down showing calls they made or received, lists of who they e-mailed or texted, links to their online banking accounts, etc."

"Damn, you are truly scary Dogbone."

"Hey, the mouse is mightier than the sword."

I touched my glass to his to show I was in agreement. He pressed on with his briefing.

"I used spyware apps in all their phones. Of course some of their phones aren't terribly sophisticated and so I wasn't able to gather as much intel from some of them."

He scrolled through several screens. He stopped at information from Dex's phone. "Okay, after you all dropped the pimp off notice the text message he sent."

I saw that Dex sent a text message to Lily, *"We need to meet – urgent."*

I sat staring at the screen. I took a sip of Pinot and rolled it around over my tongue, bathing my taste buds in the sapor of complex and subtle flavors.

"Huh, Dex and Lily." I had to really think about that.

Dogbone highlighted the response from Lily's phone. *"One hour, usual place."*

"Shit, usual place? How well does she know him?" I took another sip. "Alright, so that was last night. Are there any text's after that?"

"Nada."

"Did you follow their phones to see if they met?"

"I did. They met about one hour later at The Modicum. They stayed for a half hour in the alley beside there and then split up."

"And nothing else since then?"

"Nothing."

"Where did they go after that?"

"Dex went out pimping, you know, bouncing around to some different places. Lily went home."

"Shit. Huh, Lily and Dex? Fuck me." I took several sips of wine as my mind moved different pieces of the jigsaw puzzle around to try to see how they might fit together.

"Did he contact Petra or did he see her for any reason?"

"They were never in contact."

"Alright, how about Charlotte? Did you see any text's or phone calls involving her?"

"Yeah, on Jonathan's phone he has a few phone calls listed as connecting to hers. But that was before I imbedded the apps, so who knows what those were about?"

My mind continued to shift different people around to see the connections. I couldn't help but to stop at one point and really admire the Pinot. Damn it was good.

"What about Petra? Do you have any contacts between her and any of them since last night?"

"Not a thing."

"So Dex hasn't been in contact with Petra all day?"

"Apparently not."

"Hm, well, that's a good sign. Out of curiosity, where is Petra right now?"

"Alright, let's see." As he punched in some keys to access that information he said, "By the way, this Pinot Noir is tasty. It's nice."

"Yeah, it is isn't it."

"Okay, there you go." He turned the screen to face me. The Petra blip was at a parking area in Rock Creek Park, close to the National Zoo.

I leaned back against the bar stool, took a sip of wine and tried to think. The position was stationary, so she might have been meeting a John there or something. Dogbone and I sat staring at the screen sipping the wine. I refilled our glasses. We sat for several minutes.

"You really worried about Petra?"

"I am."

"I'll bet she had sad eyes didn't she?"

I smiled.

"Frankie, for such a mean son of a bitch you have one hell of a soft spot for big puppy dog eyes and long sad tales."

"Yeah." I took another sip. After a long moment I said, "Alright, you got anything else of significance? How about Reggie or Nancy or

Stella?"

"Well, I didn't find any connections between any of them and Stella. I had to download her connection off of your phone from when you called her the other night."

"You bugged my phone?"

"Of course."

"Asshole."

Dogbone smiled. "Stella ironically doesn't use her phone much. Most of her calls are to her work, a few to her mother and brother. It's hard to tell if she even has many friends. She has photos on the phone of her cats."

"What a nerd."

"She pretty?"

"Very."

"Prettier than Isabelle?"

"Not half as pretty as Isabelle."

"What is it with you and Isabelle man? It's the big sad eyes thing isn't it?"

I thought about Isa's eyes. "Let's move on to a different topic."

Dogbone smiled. "Okay, Nancy Dagupta, has numerous phone calls to both Jonathan and Lily. Again, this was before I set up surveillance so I have no recordings of conversations."

"Huh, Lily and Nancy? What the hell is Nancy calling Lily about?"

"You said Jonathan's into kinky sex. Maybe Lily and Jonathan actually do share more than just their street address, you know?"

"Damn, the 'Haves' certainly have a lot of little complicated games they play."

"The Haves?"

"You know, Hemingway, To Have and Have Not?"

"Ah, the Haves, yes, the ones whose lives are so well off that the only problems they have are the ones they create."

"Did you pick up anything on Rupert?"

"Yeah, he is your quintessential computer geek. The guy spends every second outside of work gaming, messaging with other gamers and trying to move to some new level in one of his war game fantasies. The guy is brilliant, but I have to say Frankie, I think this guy is oblivious to the outside world."

"Good to know."

Then Dogbone switched to show me Reggie. "You know Frankie, this one is interesting. Lots of phone calls and texts to friends. He has downloaded games and apps for a bunch of special ops type games, you know end of the world and zombie kind of bullshit."

"Is there anything that makes any little lights go off in that demented brain of yours?"

"Yeah, this is where it gets interesting. One of the people he has called several times is someone with the Chinese Embassy. Whoever the guy is he has a very secure phone that I can't stick one of these little apps into."

"So did you dig up any dirt on Reggie's

father?"

"Like you already told me, he works for the Chinese Space program, but nothing in particular pops up. There are no particular files on him in any or our national security databases. That doesn't mean he isn't doing some evil nasty communist espionage kind of dog doo, but he isn't on anybody's radar."

"Anything else on Jonathan?"

"You know, he is cagey. I think he is very aware of not using his phone to have any conversations that he doesn't want anyone to listen in on. He's cagey and smart. It's hard to tell much about him."

"You're right, it is hard to tell with him. Isabelle ran him through her databases as well, and nothing came up." I took another sip. "Well, this is all good shit Dogbone. Stay on it. I need you to pull a rabbit out of the hat for me man. Get me something I can really sink my teeth into."

"I'll work on it."

Chapter 24

Dogbone stayed in the bar and chatted and we each ate a big plate of Fiona's shepherd's pie. I noticed Fiona watching Dogbone and lingering nearby. My detective skills don't always do so well crossing over into the territory of relationships but I have deduced that she shows a keen interest in my muscled, geeky comrade. Angel is someone most women find eerily attractive in a bad boy kind of way. With Dogbone, he is so witty, chilled out and yet with such a studdly body that women just find him cute as hell. Fiona is no exception.

After Dogbone left I went upstairs, took a piss, grabbed a copy of The Ripening Sun by Patricia Atkinson and headed back down to the bar. It was 9:00.

The bar was getting really busy and Fiona was floating around like a ballroom dancer as she shuffled and spun and weaved her way between two other bartenders. Mitch was seated at the bar nursing a Jack and Coke. He was chatting with one of the evening regulars, Phyllis something. She was in her early thirties, a black woman, pretty as hell, a sharp dresser who was slender and always wore dangly earrings. The two of them were sitting close, shoulder to shoulder, chatting. The rest of the bar was crowded. It was Thursday night and Georgetown was starting to heat up.

There were no booths available so I slid in between two people on stools at the bar. Fiona noticed and came over.

"You're back. What're you having now?" She asked.

"I think I'll switch to a Syrah. Got any good ones open you are serving by the glass tonight?"

Fiona paused, looked up toward the ceiling as she thought. "Ah, I do. It's from Sonoma."

"A California Syrah sounds good."

She paused. "You alright?"

"Just contemplative," I replied.

"Looks more like morose or sullen."

"Contemplative," I emphasized.

She smiled and moved up the bar to get my drink.

Sitting and watching all the people chatting and connecting didn't help my mood. The Syrah was good. I sat and watched people for a bit as I sipped it slowly. Fiona was right, sullen was probably a better descriptor of my mood. Damn her. Sullenness can be a danger for me, which can slip into becoming maudlin if I imbibe a bit too much wine.

I pulled out my book, and for the next two and a half hours I drank wine and read. The background chatter in the bar was a pleasing distraction and I got deeply engrossed in The Ripening Sun. It's about a woman who takes over a vineyard in the Dordogne region of France, and learns to fall in step with the vines and the seasons. It's the fantasy life I secretly dream of, giving up the big city and life among the masses and criminals and degenerates, and living out my days creating wine from noble rot. The book transported me to another world and I was happy to be in it even if just for a while.

At midnight Fiona made her way over to me. As she refilled my glass she stated, "Your boys just came in."

I looked at her. "Where?"

"They are together. They just went over to a booth along the wall."

"They sitting down now?"

"Yeah."

I saw them. The one dude was huge, white, scruffy looking and wearing a big army field jacket. The smaller one was unshaven and wore a nice looking black leather jacket. He had restless dark eyes that seemed to move all around the room at one time. They sat across from each other.

One of the waitresses, Bernice, went over to their table. The little shifty one eyed her up and down and then ordered something for the both of them, holding up two fingers as he did. The big handsome guy sat there like a big dumbass, staring around. Clearly the smaller one was in charge. I took a deep breath and let it out. It felt good to be dealing with tangibles again.

I asked Fiona if she would bring me a double espresso. I wanted to be sharp and clear. Watching the two men discreetly was easy. They were so absorbed taking everything in. I kept my book in front of me and stared up over it, glancing down when their eyes came my way.

Time passed by and people started to filter out. Mitch and Phyllis left as a couple, their faces close together and smiling a lot as they went out the door. I decided I was going to come back as Mitch in my next life.

By 1:30 there were only eight people left in the place. The smaller suspect in the leather jacket came out of the booth and sat at the bar at an angle where he could watch the door. A big barkeep named Murphy went over and took his order, came back and slid a Bud Lite in front of him. The big dumbass continued to sit in the booth by himself. It was very warm in the bar and he still had his field jacket on. He looked more nervous now.

Fiona wandered over and said a little loudly, "Is there anything else I can get for you?"

I spoke softly. "Do they usually split up like that?"

"No, they usually stay together and talk."

Out of the corner of my eye I watched them as we talked. I thought for a moment.

"Give me a scotch, will ya?" I asked.

"Okay," Fiona said, eyeing me with a questioning look.

I sipped it and stared at nothing in particular. The thin guy was watching me. He was seated so that he was facing me at the far end of the bar. His eyes shifted around as he nursed his beer. The big guy had turned in the booth so his back was to the wall and he was staring out with a commanding view of the room. The little guy got up and walked to the doorway and stood there for a moment looking up and down the street. I knew this was it.

I got up and carried my tumbler of scotch with me. I acted inebriated, weaving slightly and holding the backs of chairs as I walked. Drunks are never regarded as a threat by anyone. The little guy came back into the bar and started to walk over to where Fiona was standing by the cash register. He glanced over at the big guy and nodded his head. The big guy started to slide out of the booth.

The little guy moved right past me as he stepped up to the bar. He stuck his hand inside his jacket, reaching around behind his back. The big guy reached into his field jacket at the same time.

My glass of scotch moved through the air like a bolt of lightning as I swung the sharp corner of it straight into the skinny guy's temple. His eyes fluttered and he stumbled backward. I drove the heel of my empty hand straight up under his chin like a sledgehammer, snapping his head backward. He fell like a sack of potatoes to the floor. I spun quickly, dropping to one knee, pulling out my Sig Sauer and pointing it center mass at the big guy's chest as his hand was halfway out of his jacket with a sawed off shotgun.

"Drop it dickhead!" I shouted.

He froze. He looked confused and stared down at his friend who was on the floor, not moving. He held the shotgun tightly, with it still half out of his coat as he looked me in the eyes.

"Put it down or I'll cap your ass," I said sharply through gritted teeth. Both my hands were wrapped around the handle of the Sig and I stared at him with dead calm.

He was a total dumbass and wasn't sure what to do, which made me uncertain if he was stupid enough to go for it. I spoke calmly and authoritatively. "Hey dumbass, your friend is out of it. You put the fucking gun down slowly and the two of you will just take a little ride downtown."

He lowered the shotgun and slowly set it on the floor.

"Call 911 Fiona."

When the police arrived we sat at the bar while the police officers hauled the two shit birds downtown and the cops interviewed people. I sipped another couple of glasses of scotch. Fiona sat next to me and we chatted. She laughed nervously a couple of times, out of a sense of relief. Fiona is good company, a friend. I realized looking at her that this thing with these guys had really been keeping her on edge. She was so relaxed now, almost giddy, which is not typical behavior for Fiona. It was nice to see her happy.

At one point she said, "That was a pretty nifty move with the scotch glass."

I held up the tumbler that was in my hand and said, "I've always been pretty good at handling my scotch."

She just shook her head. "I'll tell you what. Your drinks are on the house tonight."

"Thanks, then can you give me a glass of your Glenmorangie 18?"

She brought out the more expensive bottle of scotch and refilled my glass. As she did she glanced up at me and said, "It's scary how calm you were tonight when you were dealing with those two guys. How do you stay so calm? I would be scared to death."

I took a sip. It was woody, with a strong malt flavor. I looked at Fiona. "I don't know, it's just what I do."

She looked me in the eye. "You aren't scared or nervous when you deal with people like that?"

I took another sip and held it in my mouth as I thought about it. "Hm, I don't really know."

"How can you not know if you're scared?"

"I get a kind of tunnel vision when I am looking someone in the eye. You know Angel sits a long way off, removed from it all most of the time. I am always up close and personal, staring into their eyes, waiting to see if they have the balls or are stupid enough to go for it." I took another sip. "At times like that everything is very clear in your mind. You don't have time to think or worry. You just stand right on the edge, your mind clear as a bell, waiting."

"Waiting for what?"

"To kill 'em, if it comes to that."

Fiona stared at me as if she wasn't quite sure she really knew me. "Does it ever bother you, afterwards I mean?"

I tilted the rest of the glass up and downed the contents in one big quaff. I set the glass down and said, "If it did, I wouldn't be much good at my job, would I?"

I pushed away from the bar and headed upstairs.

Chapter 25

I had a hell of a headache when I woke up. I slept past 11:00. It took a full couple of minutes to remember what had transpired at the bar last night. I pulled on some jeans, a t-shirt and my cowboy boots and went downstairs. The smell of coffee and various meats cooking filled my nostrils as I scooted up to the bar. Fiona saw me and brought a thick mug over and filled it with steaming hot coffee. She looked so awake and bubbly. God it was nauseating.

"Mornin' Frank."

"Is it?" I said.

She was beaming from ear to ear. It was too damn much.

"You were really something last night."

"That's what all the ladies tell me," I said.

She ignored my stupid comment.

"So, what will it be today? It's on the house, whatever you want."

"Uh, just coffee for now."

"I know what you need, Eggs Benedict and a Bloody Mary."

"Oh god."

Mitch was standing at the bar with a Jack and Coke in his hand. He was standing very erect, sipping. I looked over at him.

"Damn Mitch, don't you have anything else to do?" My inhibitions were at their lowest point. I was on a roll.

"You're in quite a mood this morning," Mitch replied, taking another sip.

"I have a hell of a hangover."

"That's what this is good for," he noted, holding up his glass.

"I saw you leave with Phyllis last night." He didn't comment. Good for him. "She's pretty," I added.

He still didn't comment. Fiona came out and brought the carafe over and topped off my coffee.

"Hey Mitch, did you hear what Frank did last night?" She asked.

"No, what'd he do?"

"He kicked the shit out of two guys who were going to rob the place. Hit the one guy right in the head with his scotch glass."

"I wish I had been here to see that," Mitch

said. "Here's to you Frank." He lifted his glass in my direction.

I lifted me coffee mug in return.

"You're still in pretty damn good shape for an older guy," Mitch said.

I gave him the finger.

"I meant that as a compliment."

"Sure you did," I said.

"Damn, I can't believe I missed you in action. Seriously Frank, that's very cool."

"Thanks."

"Who were they?"

Fiona jumped in. "You know those two guys who have been coming in a lot the last week or so, right around closing time? One's a huge football player type and the other one is a wiry greaser?"

"Oh yeah, I saw those guys. Damn, so they actually tried to hold you up?"

"Yeah."

"You been held up before?"

"Once, that's when I offered the apartment upstairs to Frank. He's my watchdog."

"Frank the watchdog." Mitch said the title outloud, like he was testing to see how it sounded.

"Hm, well, I have never been called a watchdog. I've been called a dirty dog by a lot of people, but never a watchdog," I added.

"He's so damn modest," Fiona said and

damn if she didn't grab my cheek and pinch it hard as hell. Why do people do that?

"Damn Fiona," I exclaimed.

"Oh, sorry Frank."

My phone beeped. I looked at it, Isabelle. I smiled. I figured she had checked the police reports this morning and knew about what happened last night. I answered the phone.

"Frank, you alright?"

"Hey sweetie, yeah, I'm good."

"I read the police report."

"I figured you did."

"What the hell were you doing? You could have got yourself killed?" She was pissed.

"Those guys were dipshits. Believe me, I was in no danger."

"Don't bullshit me Frank Goulet."

"Alright, they were the meanest sons of bitches since Al Capone, how's that?"

"Stop," she said more softly. "I, I was just worried about you."

"I know. Seriously, thanks for calling, but I'm fine."

She laughed nervously. "I should have you come down to the courthouse and do a little cleaning up down here like you did with those guys. We have some sleazy defense attorneys that could use some slapping around."

"I've seen you go after some of those bastards in court. You seem to bitch slap them all over the courtroom just fine on your own."

She laughed. "Are you really alright Frank?"

"Yeah, I am."

"Okay, well, I just you know, wanted to call and make sure you were okay." She sounded almost bashful.

"Thanks."

"Okay, well, I uh, I guess I better go."

"Alright, hey, really Isa, thanks for calling."

"Well, I….." she stopped and I knew what she came a hair away from saying. Then she said, "Well, anyway, I just really care about you, you know?"

I smiled. "Yeah, I do know."

"Okay, well, I gotta go."

"Go get those bad guys."

She hung up. I sat staring at the phone. When I looked up Fiona was staring at me.

"What?"

"I do not understand what the hell is going on with you and Isabelle." She shook her head, looking annoyed and turned and walked back into the kitchen.

Just then my phone beeped again. I picked it up. "This is Frank."

"It's Ted. We got a ransom note this morning asking for 50 million dollars in cash for the return of the briefcase."

"Huh, a note? Is it on paper or electronic?"

"On paper."

"Where'd you find it?"

"It was under the windshield wiper blade of my Mercedes when I came out to go to work."

"Has Jonathan seen it?"

"Yeah, I called him first thing and we met and looked at it. I'm in his office downtown."

I looked at my watch, 12:04. "I'll be there in twenty minutes."

Chapter 26

I didn't bother to change. I just grabbed my leather jacket, keys, wallet and gun and headed out to my car. I was sitting in Jonathan's office in 19 minutes. Jonathan handed me the note.

"Your briefcase is intact. I can't say as much for the delivery girl. Just so you know, for verification, there are four files inside the briefcase, along with two computer discs, notes from three meetings at Aberdeen Proving Grounds, along with chemical formulas for the ceramics. None of your files have been shared YET. You can get it back for $50,000,000 with a wire transfer to a Grand Cayman account. You have until this evening to respond and then three days to pull it together. I have other

bidders.

If I don't hear from you by 7:00 p.m. I will sell it to your competitors. Respond by hanging a red towel in the window of Jonathan's downtown office by 4:00 this afternoon. After that I will be in touch."

The note was computer generated and printed out. I turned the note over in my hands. The paper looked clean.

"What do you think?" Jonathan asked.

"It's to the point," I said.

"Do you think it's legit?"

"You tell me. The person mentioned the contents of the briefcase. Was the description of the contents accurate?"

"It was," Jonathan stated.

"Hm," I uttered, staring down at the note.

"What should we do?" Ted asked.

"Does your company have that kind of money?"

"We do," Ted said.

"Well, how much does it mean to you?"

"We have to get the information back. This project is solid gold. This is a real break-through in ceramic technology and could develop into multiple government contracts for aerospace and nuclear applications," Ted said.

"What if they have copied everything and sell the rest of it anyway?" I asked.

Jonathan looked surprised. "I mean, what else are we going to do?"

"I assume those files aren't your only copies," I noted.

"Of course not, but we have to try to get it back to keep it from leaking out," Jonathan said.

"Well, I would say hang the red towel in the window. By the way, can I take this note? I want to have some forensics people take a look at it?"

I noticed no one mentioned the comment on the girl. I added, "They did suggest here that the girl who stole it from you is either hurt or worse."

"Serves the little bitch right for stealing it from me," Jonathan stated.

"Fair enough, I'm sure I'd feel the same way," I commented.

Ted looked like he was ready to burst.

"What's on your mind Ted?" I asked.

"Goddamn it Frank, we are paying you a fortune to catch these people and recover our data. Haven't you turned up anything?"

"Very little. Whoever was behind it is smart."

"Do you think it's Dexter Deahl and Charlotte acting together?" Jonathan asked.

"Dex grew up on the streets, been in and out of prison, beat several raps. He's street smart, but he is disorganized, can't even cash checks people give him. No, look at how well thought out this note is written. This didn't come from somebody like Dex or Charlotte.

This was written by someone with very organized thoughts," I said.

"You don't think Dex is smart enough?"

"He's street smart, which counts for a lot, but this whole thing is too well planned and executed for someone as disorganized as him."

"So do you have anyone who is your main suspect?"

"I have several working hypothesizes," I stated.

"Well do you have one that is your main hypothesis that you can chase down? We gotta get something going here Frank."

"You don't ever box yourself into a corner or gamble with theories. Deduction is a science. You develop your theories based on facts, not speculation. We will catch them," I stated calmly.

When I said that, Ted turned red in the face. He looked like his head was going to explode. "Damn!" He blurted out. He stood up and started pacing.

Jonathan leaned back in his chair, put his elbows on the arms of his chair and placed his fingertips together, studying me. "You think this person is really smart?"

"I do."

"Then what makes you so sure you will catch them?"

"I will catch them."

"Well, then do you mind sharing what

your theories are so far?"

"I do."

He sat staring at me with a look on his face as if I had just slapped him again. "You work for me Frank. I want to know what you have uncovered."

"I will let you know when I have narrowed it down."

"I could fire you Frank," Jonathan said.

"That's your prerogative Jonathan. If that's what you want to do then go ahead and just pay me what you owe me to date."

Jonathan and I sat staring at each other. He wasn't used to anyone telling him what to do or not getting his way. I was immoveable. I didn't care if he fired me or not and so I had nothing to lose. A man with nothing to lose has all the edge. I sat smiling. Finally, Jonathan's face broadened into a smile.

"You are quite brazen Frank." He smiled. "I like that."

"I am also damn good at what I do. I will find out what happened Jonathan and I will find Charlotte. She is the key. She wasn't in this alone, and she is the one person who can tell us who else was involved."

"But can you find out in time, before we have to pay the ransom?" Ted asked.

"Even if I don't, we can find whoever is involved afterward and recover everything."

Ted looked sick with worry. I didn't

really give a shit about how he felt. My job wasn't to make him or Jonathan feel good. And it sure as hell wasn't to hold their hands. It was to recover the briefcase and quite frankly no one was above suspicion at this point, particularly people closest to the heart of it all.

"How close are you to finding Charlotte?" Jonathan asked.

"Damn close." I lied. "When we find her, we find out who hired her, ergo, we find out who has the briefcase."

Jonathan sat thinking about that. "Alright Frank. We'll see if you really are as good as Dani says you are."

Ted had taken a seat and was leaning forward, his elbows on the arms of the chair and his head buried deeply in his hands. He was rocking slightly back and forth. "Oh my god, oh my god, $50,000,000. It's almost all we have in our accounts. This is going to bust us. Shit."

"That's almost all you have in liquid assets?" I asked.

"It is," he stated.

"Huh," was all I could muster. The ransoming person must have known the amount of their liquid assets.

"Alright, well, for now we'll put the towel in the window and we will need to arrange the wire transfer," Jonathan said.

"Damn, $50 million. God, that is going to devastate us financially," Ted said.

"What else are we going to do Ted? They have us by the balls. We have to pay," Jonathan said.

Ted got up from his chair and went over to a small bar that was in Jonathan's office and poured himself a tall gin and tonic. He seemed truly lost, devastated. He turned around with the drink in his hand. "God Jon, this is going to ruin us. That means no more money for R and D. We can't afford to give them $50 million in cash. Our shareholders will find out what happened and then they will dump our stock."

"We have the money," Jonathan said.

"We do. We do. But it will take almost everything we have in cash assets," Ted said. "What if you and I both put in $10 million of our own cash just to help make it? We can recoop the cost over the next few years."

"Out of our own personal accounts? Are you crazy? God Ted," Jonathan was staring at Ted as if he was from another planet.

"Jon, we have poured our hearts and souls into building this company. I mean, look, $10 million isn't going to break either one of us, and when we get this prototype up and running we will make a goddamn fortune that will make it all worth it." Ted spoke with such passion. He had a real sparkle in his eye. It was impressive. It made me realize why Jonathan kept him on board. The guy was a diehard, a stoic.

"Ted, don't be a fool. There are no

guarantees. I believe in this as much as you do but we have been busting our asses for the last couple of years and we are still a good ways off from this becoming a reality. Hell, we haven't been able to work out the kinks, and there's no guarantee we will. Plus, we have other good solid projects and two patents. We'll be alright." He paused, then added, "Besides, what if these guys really have sold the plans to someone else. For all we know they are negotiating with some other buyer right now. God, if they do that whatever we put in is toast. We're dead in the water financially."

I have to admit, as much as I was ready to drink the Kool Aid after Ted's speech, I had to admit, Jonathan was dead on balls accurate. "Look," I said. "I know my two cents may not be worth much, but Jonathan's right. There is no reason to believe these guys are playing it straight with you. You could give them the money and then get screwed anyway. Are you're other projects really enough to buoy you up?"

"They can carry us some, but what got people to really start investing was this new ceramic technology," Ted said. He then walked over to his chair and fell into it. His face was ashen. "God, all of our work, all of our goddamn work." He sat staring at the floor.

Chapter 27

When I left Jonathan and Ted I decided to follow up on something. I hopped in my car and headed back to the Spurrier's residence.

Judging from Dogbone's surveillance, Lily was tied into this much more than I had originally suspected. And her ties to Dexter Deahl were eating at me. Finding Charlotte was key. And if everything I had learned was true the odds of Charlotte stealing from Dex seemed slim, which made it seem more likely he was involved. Lily's ties to both of them were becoming more incriminating than ever. I had to know what Lily knew.

Maria answered the door and I waited for Lily in the huge hallway.

"Frank, I was so hoping you would come

back to see me," Lily said as she entered the room carrying a martini in her hand. Clearly she was getting an early start on the day. She was in a red satin robe that was open all the way down to the sash which was only loosely holding it all together.

"Lily, I hope you don't mind. I was dying to see the Bogdanoves again and I wanted to ask you a few follow up questions anyway."

She turned to Maria. "Maria, would you serve us martinis in the solarium?"

I turned to Maria, "Do you have any scotch or wine?"

"Si senor, we have both," she replied.

"What kind of wine do you have?" I asked.

Lily cut in, "We have a whole wine seller Frank, full of the best wines. What kind would you like?"

Never one to pass up an opportunity I said, "Do you have some type of nice Burgundy or even a Cote Rotie?"

"You certainly know your wines." Lily took a sip or her martini and then turned to Maria. "Get Senor Goulet a bottle of the Clos du Vougeot."

"You are a gracious hostess."

She smiled up at me playfully with a seductive look, slipped her arm through mine and said, "Maybe I can get you drunk and take advantage of you."

"I think you already have taken advantage of me."

She pulled her head back slightly and pretended to look hurt. "Frank I am shocked you think I would do anything to hurt such a sexy man as you."

"Let's just say you may not have been completely honest with me."

"This is Washington, what can I say?"

She tugged gently on my arm, coaxing me toward the solarium. I fell in pace beside her as we walked that way. I stared at a Robert Henri painting that was on the wall as we passed it while Lily sipped her martini.

"Oh Frank, you and I could have such a wonderful time together. You know Jonathan won't be home until late tonight."

"What did you have in mind, a game of Monopoly?"

She laughed and stopped walking. "You are naughty. Here I am practically throwing myself at you. What more can a woman do?"

"Practically throwing yourself at me?" I said with a smile. "Lily, in truth, you would be utterly disappointed if I said yes."

"I would?"

I stared down at her and smiled, "You would get bored my lovely Lily. I'm too old fashioned and still need to get in the mood over a good dinner, and a bottle of Bordeaux or Barolo while we listen to Stan Getz."

She looked up at me skeptically, "You are very smooth Frank."

"Like a good Bordeaux."

She narrowed her eyes and smiled up at me. "Ooh, one of these days I would like to get you good and drunk and see if what you are saying is true. Something tells me that a man who lives as dangerously as you do probably makes love just as dangerously."

"Believe me, I am utterly boring." I stared down at her, meeting her gaze with a smile.

"Oh alright Frank, enough of this dribble. Come into the solarium and ask me what you will and we will see if perhaps the wine can loosen you up a bit," she bantered.

As she turned to lead me into the solarium I uttered a quiet sigh of relief. I knew with Lily this was only partly a game for her overly indulgent and bored lifestyle, but she was a lonely woman and it seemed likely that she had played this game before of the seductress with the hired help. I could only imagine a handsome cable guy coming in to wire the house and getting more than a handwritten check before it was all over.

We sat down at the same table where we sat before. Maria arrived with a bottle of Clos du Vougeot, already uncorked. I picked up the bottle and glass and greedily poured myself a small amount, listening to the gurgling sound as the deep purple liquid filled the glass.

Maria set another martini down on the table beside Lily. Lily tossed her head back and downed the remainder of the one in her hand, set down the empty glass and picked up the fresh one in one long, unbroken motion. As she sipped it she watched me swirl the deep colored liquid around in my glass and sniff it.

"You wine snobs take way too long to drink. I can put down two to three martinis by the time you have swirled your glass around, sniffed it repeatedly and then talked about it to death."

"Oh Lily, see, drinking your way is like sex without the foreplay. The sniffing, looking, appreciating, it all titillates your senses. It enhances the overall experience."

She held her martini up to me by way of a toast and said, "Foreplay Frank, is way overrated."

"Not to everyone," I countered, holding my glass up to return her toast. We both took a sip.

"Alright Frank, well, since we clearly aren't going to have any afternoon delight, you might as well tell me what you came here to discuss."

I took a sip of wine, let the velvety texture linger on my taste buds, then let it slide down my throat. It was good. Then I said, "I'm here to talk about Dexter Deahl."

She took a sip and stared at me. I stared back.

"Dexter Deahl, go on," she said.

"You met with Dexter the other night."

"No, I didn't." She took another sip.

I looked into her eyes and took another long sip and let it linger as I stared at her. I swallowed. She continued to stare at me with utter conviction. "So you didn't meet Dexter Deahl in the alley beside The Modicum Hotel?"

"No, why?"

I was seeing a hard, tough side of Lily I had not seen before.

"Do you call Dexter to set up soirees?"

"Yes." She sipped again.

Monosyllabic responses were not like Lily. Her eyes seemed more catlike now as we talked, suspicious and alert.

"For you or Jonathan?"

"Sometimes Jon has me call for him."

"Do you ever call for yourself?"

She was staring me directly in the eyes the whole time she was talking to me. "For the two of us. I told you before, Jonathan likes to sometimes have other ladies do things with us."

"Oh, that's right, you did say that."

She was guarded now. This was good. Something was needling her. If putting people at ease during questioning doesn't work then I like to needle them, see what buttons I can push.

"Tell me about Charlotte."

"What's to tell?"

"How well do you know her?"

"Somewhat."

"Have you slept with her?"

"Jonathan had her sleep with us several times."

"Have you ever called her or gotten together with her on your own?"

Lily sipped her martini and just stared at me.

"Have you?"

"Yes."

"Did you take your husband's briefcase Lily?"

"No."

"Let me rephrase that. Did you have Charlotte take your husband's briefcase?"

She took another sip.

"What if I did Frank?"

"Then I would say I don't blame you one damn bit. Your husband is an asshole who neglects you and sleeps with other women right under your nose."

She broke eye contact for the first time. She looked past me, out the windows of the solarium to some distant spot far beyond the glass walls of her gilded cage. She took a sip of her martini and remained silent, lost in her thoughts.

She turned back to look at me. "Would Charlotte be in trouble for taking it, if she did do it?"

"It depends."

She reached over for her pack of cigarettes on the table beside her. She slid one out, set it between her lips, stared at the tip of it as she lit it and inhaled deeply. She leaned her head back and slowly blew the smoke up toward the glass ceiling.

After a long moment she looked me in the eyes and said, "Were there any other questions Frank?"

"Did you have Charlotte take your husband's briefcase?"

She looked me dead in the eyes and said nothing.

"Lily, I think your husband is a turd, but I have a job to do."

"My husband deserves whatever happens to him."

"Lily, honestly, I don't want to see you hurt. Not just from a legal stand point. I like you Lilly."

"Why do you like me Frank?"

"Something tells me that you and I are not so different."

"If that's why you like me then that's rather narcissistic."

I smiled. "I have always been my biggest fan."

The look in her eyes turned more serious. "If you like me Frank, then sleep with me."

I wish I could say that this gorgeous woman was offering herself up to me because I just have that kind of effect on women, but I just don't. Lily was in deep shit and she was looking for rubber boots to pull on so she could step out of it. She knew one of her aces in the hole was always exactly the card she was playing right now.

"Not a good idea Lily."

She set her martini down, snubbed out her cigarette and stood up. Her right hand pulled at her sash. Her robe opened. It revealed black sheer lace panties. She stood staring at me. God she was stunning.

I stood up. "No Lily."

She moved across the room and stopped directly in front of me. She stared up into my eyes and reached up slowly with her right hand and touched my lips with her fingertips. Lily was such a sensual creature.

"Lily, I said no."

Her hand flashed through the air and I caught her wrist right before her open palm reached my face.

"I said no," I growled.

She jerked her hand free and spun away from me, heading over to the table. Keeping her back to me she reached for the cigarette pack, slipped one out and lit it. She inhaled, leaned her head back and blew it out hard. Spinning around to face me she had a smile on her face.

Slowly she walked toward me, taking another pull on her cigarette, her robe was open in front and her hips swayed as she approached.

"You Frank, are a very bad boy. You know you work for hubby, so in a manner of speaking, you work for me." She paused in front of me.

"Lily, I am not a cop anymore. If what is going on here is some little spat between you and your hubby, I really don't give a shit. But if you or anyone else has stolen classified information and are using it to get back at someone to prove a point, or if people like Ted Freen are going to lose huge sums of money to pay for your little vendetta, these are the things I do give a shit about."

I looked down at her. There was pure hatred in her eyes.

"You know where Charlotte is don't you?" I asked.

She turned away from me and stood stockstill.

"Do you love Charlotte Lily?"

She took another drag and stood staring off into the distance.

"Do you know what is going on Lily? Did you have Charlotte take Jonathan's briefcase."

Without turning around, in a faraway voice she said, "I can't say anything Frank."

I stared at her a long moment. There was

so much anger and resentment in her it was practically oozing out of her pores. She wasn't talking. I turned and left her standing there.

Chapter 28

I sat behind the wheel of my car trying to get my head around what was going on. I started the engine and on my drive back I turned right on M Street instead of heading straight back to the apartment. I passed through Georgetown and the hordes that crowded the streets busily going about their business. I thought of whatever pain was torturing Lily. I passed the turn for Key Bridge and headed north on MacArthur Boulevard, paralleling the C&O Canal straight out of town. I downshifted and punched the accelerator. I pulled left and shot around two cars in front of me, hopping over the double yellow line and shooting past them like a rocket. One of the cars honked their horn. I didn't give a shit. The speedometer hit 80 as I flew up the two lane boulevard.

What the hell was going on with Lily? If she was masterminding this whole thing then she was using Charlotte, either with the help of Dex or on her own. According to Petra, Charlotte loved Jonathan. Charlotte was a product of the street though, like Dex, people like that show far more allegiance to money than they do to their belief in fairytales.

Lily had been about the same age as Charlotte when Jonathan fell for her. Was there a part of her that was trying to remove Charlotte from his grasp and his influence? It would be a doubly powerful blow to Jonathan.

I downshifted, punched the accelerator and swerved around another car in the roadway. They honked at me as well. I was feeling crazy as I sped up the road. God, Petra and Lily, two ball-bustingly gorgeous women standing there in front of me, offering themselves to me, what the hell was wrong with me? Angel would have enjoyed himself, taken advantage of it. I couldn't. I'm too obsessive with my cases. I never let anyone or anything too close who might interfere with my investigations. I pulled around another car and punched the gas, sending the speedometer up to 93.

I suddenly came up on the traffic light at Arizona Avenue. I swung a hard right, shooting up the narrow road toward Cathedral Heights. I had to slow down as I hit traffic.

It was sunny outside and the air smelled clean and fresh and my head began to clear ever so slightly as I drove on. I nosed my way up Arizona and turned right onto Nebraska. I continued up toward Tenleytown. I felt like I should just continue on that road and head straight for the Psychiatric Institute of Washington and go in and get my head examined. But instead I swung a right onto Massachusetts and headed toward the National Cathedral.

Eventually I turned back onto Wisconsin and headed back toward Fiona's. The little outing had at least calmed me down, but I felt restless and antsy. I wished in a way that I had slept with Lily now. Why the hell didn't I? Even if she was the one behind it she was doing it to her husband because he was a piece of shit who treated her as if she was an even bigger piece of shit. And all of this angst was over some secrets for a fucking little piece of ceramic. God I felt like I was going nuts.

Back at the apartment I touched base with Dogbone. He said he had a break. So I set up a little powwow to meet with him and Angel in the bar.

I went downstairs just after 4:00 and Fiona's was already about 30% packed with patrons hammering down their drinks like a bunch of carpenters trying to wrap things up on a Friday afternoon. There was one booth available along the wall, next to the booth where the two shit birds had been sitting which I had taken down just the night before. I slid my ass onto the bench facing the door so I could watch for Angel and Dogbone. Fiona saw me sit down and came around the bar.

As she approached the table I said, "So are my little heroics from last night still buying me free drinks?"

She looked down at me with her flaming red halo of hair framing that fiery Irish face. "Freebies are over."

"Oh well, all good things must come to an end."

"How are you doing Frank?" She said it sincerely.

"I'm doing okay."

She stared at me a long moment.

"Why do you ask?"

"I don't know Frank, you seem distracted, tired, edgy."

"Are you doing the bartender shrink thing?"

"I'm just making an observation Frank, as a friend."

"Well thanks."

Then her normal cold, savvy, streetwise look returned. "Look, I just don't wanna knock on your door one day because there is the stench of three day old Frank coming out from under the door because you blew your brains out."

I smiled. "Yeah, I thought it was something touching like that."

I ordered a Reuben and a Beck's. She made some comment about how original that was. As she disappeared into the back I thought about her question.

I was tired. This whole thing with dirt bags like Jonathan and the hookers, the pricks like Dex and all the power hungry smug bastards in their Armani worlds, really made me wonder if it was time to give it up. For more than two decades I had been cleaning shit up on the streets, and just like any street cleaner I would return the next day to find it was just as dirty. What the hell difference did it make? There were still a million Jonathan's and Dex's out there exploiting lost kids and treating people like Lily and Stella like shit. Jonathan, what a worthless piece of shit. Then my mind drifted back to that judge's ruling, letting the Independence Avenue stalker go and the two teenagers who died. That was one of those haunting memories that was never far from my mind and at times like this it made my naturally sunny disposition more somber and withdrawn.

Fiona brought out my Reuben right as Dogbone and Angel walked into the pub. I waved and they came over. They looked like Mutt and Jeff. Angel cut such an enormous figure when he entered a room. Beside him was Dogbone with his dark skin and his dark shifty eyes which were always in motion, scanning everything around him.

"Yo Frank," Dogbone called out, opening his arms wide as he stepped up to the table.

I rose up from the bench and stepped up to give him a bear hug. We embraced. I stepped back and looked at him. "Damn, I didn't notice the other day how much you've trimmed down."

"It's all that good livin' man. Remaining a bachelor, abstaining from having sex more than once a night and limiting myself to no more than a 12 pack a day."

"You are so disciplined. I have always admired your iron will when it comes to drinking and sex," I said with a laugh. We released one another and I offered my hand to Angel. He smiled and his giant paw wrapped around mine.

"Hey bro, that mine?" Angel asked, pointing at my Reuben. I could see the hungry look in his eyes.

"I am armed and dangerous, so don't even think about going for that sandwich," I warned.

Right then Fiona stepped up. "Hey Angel, Dogbone."

"Hey Fi," Angel said with a big smile. He leaned over and gave her a peck on the cheek.

"What're you boys havin' today?"

Angel said, "Start bringing out Coronas

two at a time for Dogbone and me, and refresh them about every fifteen minutes."

Fiona smiled.

The two of them sat down across from me and I gathered up my sandwich and sunk my teeth into it. As I was chewing I said, "So, you got anything new Dogbone?"

He set his laptop on the table, flipped open the lid and turned it on. He watched me eat while the computer booted up. "Damn that Reuben looks good."

"It's the best." I took another bite and chased it with a swig of Beck's.

Fiona stepped up to the table at that moment and placed the Coronas in front of the guys. She could see we were busy so she turned to go, but not without a quick glance at Dogbone. He was so absorbed in looking at the computer he didn't notice.

Dogbone took a sip of his Corona and then turned the computer screen at an angle so we all could see it. "Last night, I was pulling a late nighter with a lady friend and I got up to take a piss. While I did I checked the computer. There was a phone call to Lily's phone from Charlotte, she also called Dex."

I thought of the pained look in Lily's eyes as she told me that she couldn't tell me what was going on.

"Where the hell has Charlotte been all this time?" Angel asked.

"Well, it's possible she had her phone off all this time, which would explain why I couldn't connect with it to try to install an app."

"Do you know where she is?" I asked.

"Whoa, hold on, we'll get there. Notice, Charlotte tried Lily's phone and there was no answer. She left a message that simply said, 'Call me.' Then she disconnected and called Dex. Dex immediately cut her off and told her to hang up and he would see her shortly."

I stared at his computer screen. "He'll see her shortly? What the fuck is going on?" As I stared at the computer screen I took another bite of the sandwich. It was warm and rich and tangy.

"So where the hell is she?" I asked as I chewed.

"Right here," Dogbone stated, pointing to a blip on the screen.

"She's in Chantilly? Shit, she is just around the corner from where the SPURRIER AND FREEN research lab is. Like, maybe ten minutes away," I noted.

I glanced up at Angel. He lifted his eyebrows at me and nodded his head up and down showing he was liking what he was hearing.

"Is it a house?"

"It is."

A little light bulb lit up in my head. "You know what it's also close to? Dulles Airport."

"Huh, interesting coincidence," Dogbone noted.

We all sat in silence for a moment and stared at the printout.

"You did tell Dex to find Charlotte. You think he found her and is now somehow negotiating something with Lily about her? It sounds like Lily likes Charlotte as much as Jonathan," Dogbone said.

"It's more than that as far as Lily goes. She loves Charlotte and she definitely knows where she is," I chimed in.

"You know that?" Dogbone asked.

"Petra told me and then I confirmed it when I met with Lily."

"Okay, well maybe Dex is in cahoots with Lily in this whole thing," Dogbone stated.

"Hm, I always love that word cahoot," I stated. "Anyway, it's true, they could be cahooting."

"Is cahooting a word?" Dogbone asked.

"Well cahoot is," I replied.

"I know but I'm not sure you can technically use the word cahoot that way. I think you have to say something like they are in cahoots, not they are cahooting."

"Huh." I paused to think about that.

"Who gives a fuck?" Angel said.

"Hey, if we are going to sound professional then we need to make sure we don't use incorrect, out dated or false terminology. It takes a little of the shine off our image," Dogbone said.

I smiled at Dogbone. "He's such a perfectionist", I stated. "Alright, well for now we will not use cahooting, only cahoot."

"Fair enough," he said.

Angel looked back and forth between us. He downed his Corona and looked around for Fiona. "Oh my god, I need another goddamn beer."

Right as he said that Fiona was approaching. Angel looked at her and said, "Forget the every fifteen minutes rule. This is an emergency. I need two more right now."

Fiona smiled. "I'll be right back."

"Hey big boy," I said to Angel, "You wanna go outside and play on the jungle gym while the adults talk here or what?"

"Hey fuck all this technical lingo and bullshit about terminology. Just tell me who you want me to shoot or what to blow up and let me deal with that shit."

I shook my head and exchanged glances with Dogbone. He laughed. We both leaned back in our chairs and sipped our beers.

"So, Dex and Lily?" Dogbone stated to nobody in particular.

"Maybe," I said. "But it is totally possible that Lily is acting as a go between with Dex, trying to protect Charlotte. Hell, maybe Lily knew where she was all along and Dex is trying to get her to give Charlotte up."

"You think Lily was using Charlotte to help her blackmail Jonathan?"

I took another sip of beer. "It's possible. Lily is smart and has years' worth of pent up anger and resentment toward Jonathan. Of course it's also possible that after Charlotte took the briefcase she ran to Lily for protection from Dex or whoever the main perpetrator is."

"I'm not gonna lie, Lily is looking stronger in my mind as being the main perp," Dogbone stated. "You said she's got motive and is smart as hell."

"Yes on both counts," I replied.

I took another bite of my Reuben and looked over at Angel who was sucking hard on his Corona and watching a pretty woman in a tight black dress as she entered the building.

"Hey, you following all this big boy?" I asked.

"Whatever," he said taking another swig. "Just tell me who to shoot."

I laughed.

We all sat back and downed a few more beers as the sun went down and the street lights came on along M Street. We got loud and started talking about the good old days. Fiona even came over and joined us at one point. She and Dogbone joked and ribbed each other mercilessly. I thought she and Dogbone actually looked good together. Fiona never took any shit off anyone and could be really funny once she let her hair down. Dogbone was funny as hell and never seemed to let anything bother him. I knew Fiona didn't date much, if at all. I figured when this was over I would try to set the two of them up on a date.

Chapter 29

The next morning I got a phone call that Jonathan and Ted received another note. I went to their office around lunch time. Ted looked like he hadn't slept. Jonathan looked like his normal self, completely self-absorbed and unaffected by it all.

"So, where's the note?" I asked.

Ted handed it to me. I took it and sat down in a big overstuffed chair. It read,

"I see you are willing to deal, good boys. When we make the exchange I will give you an account number for an account in a Grand Cayman bank. I want to see the money wired in there before I make the exchange.

In order to prove that I have what I say I have

there is one of the computer discs from the briefcase
included with this note. It is not the most important
data, but it proves I have the case.

Be at your research lab on Monday at 10:30
a.m. I want to see only Jonathan present, no one else.
Tell the rest of the employees to take the day off. If
anyone else shows up with him the briefcase goes to
the next highest bidder. I expect Ted Freen to be at
the bank awaiting your call so he can make the
transaction. "

Sincerely, ...

"Well," I stated. "Interesting."

"Did you take the other note we received
to your friends in forensics?" Ted asked.

"Yeah, but they don't have anything yet
and I doubt they will find much. Whoever this
is, they are very thorough and smart."

I looked over at Jonathan. He was
leaning back in his chair deep in thought, with
his fingertips touching together in front of him.
It reminded me what Ted said about Jonathan
being an exceptional chess player. He looked
like he was in a game of it right now.

"Jonathan?"

He looked up. "Yes?"

"You seem to be deep in thought. You
have anything you can add?"

"No, I just can't think who would be
doing this. I have to admit, of all the people we

have dealt with in the last couple of years who had something to be angry about and who knew our company and what was in our research, the one who comes to mind is Stella Buccino. She's smart as hell. And she knew what kind of budgets we worked with and might have some idea how much we were good for."

I took a deep breath and let it out, studying Jonathan. "You really think she's capable of something like this?"

"She is a brilliant woman, brilliant. I think she could do anything she wanted to and she has been jilted. A jilted woman is a dangerous woman," he said.

"Jilted? Interesting choice of words," I said. "You're not saying this because she refused to sleep with you and so you are harboring feelings of resentment?"

He looked at me over his fingertips. He smiled, looking smug and amused, "Jilted by this company Frank. As far as sexually, Stella is a gorgeous woman. She's hot. But a stuck up bitch like her is probably frigid anyway. Don't get me wrong, I would love to have tapped into that. But, I have had far better looking and far more willing ladies. But right now we are talking money and business. And I'll be damned if I am going to let anyone steal what we have worked so hard for. I'm telling you, Stella is brilliant. Don't underestimate her."

"I never underestimate anyone, but I

spoke with Stella. She is working on things that are completely different. You think she would risk her career like this?" I asked.

"She feels that her work, what she created, was stolen from her. You don't think she wants retribution? As far as her career? We are talking about $50,000,000 Frank. She wouldn't need a career if she had that kind of money. She could go anywhere, do anything. Plus, she would know she got us back for stealing her idea and cutting her out of the research and the glory of it."

"She doesn't strike me as being someone who is in her work for the glory. She seems proud to be a part of a team, one of a group," I stated, thinking that Jonathan probably couldn't comprehend what it was like to enjoy the feeling of teamwork. He was so completely egotistical, all about himself, his own glory and wealth. Even with Ted, his devoted and faithful minion, he seemed like he really didn't give a shit. It seemed hard to fathom, like the Lone Ranger not giving a damn about Tanto. It was hard to comprehend.

"Don't be fooled Frank. She is a vain woman. All women are vain. They spend hours everyday staring at themselves in mirrors. They are always checking other women out, buying clothes to outdo them. Their lives are vanity."

I was listening to him say this and looking at this eye liner wearing playboy who's whole life was about conquests of women and made himself out to be responsible for his whole company's rise to prominence when he had people under him doing all the real research and development. Yet here he was saying that all women were vain.

I got up from my chair.

"Where are you going?"

"I have work to do."

"You work for me. Your work is right here," Jonathan said.

"No, your work is pulling together the funds. My work is doing everything possible to catch the son of a bitch before you have to do the wire transfer, or catching them after the fact. And the longer I sit here the less time I have to be out banging on doors."

Jonathan considered that. "Alright, you may go," he said, giving me a flip of his hand, dismissing me the way a Lord might dismiss a servant from a room.

Chapter 30

I had a hell of a lot of ground to cover
before the exchange was made. True to my
European upbringing, I decided to start with
dinner. In truth, I needed to see Stella again. I
honestly didn't know what to think of the whole
Dex, Lily and Charlotte thing. Charlotte had
obviously taken the briefcase, but for all I knew
Lily and Dex were hiding her now from
Jonathan. Maybe Dex wanted one of his best
ladies back in action or Lily wanted her all to
herself. She was clearly in love with Charlotte
and wanted to protect her. As far as Stella,
Jonathan's comments were bullshit. There was
no way Stella was involved. I could totally
understand Jonathan's suspicions about her. She
had a great motive for doing it. I just didn't

believe his suspicions were justified. But I had to follow up.

We met for dinner at a Restaurant in Old Town Alexandria. It was a Tapas restaurant, serving old style Spanish food. It was Friday night and their Flamenco band and dancer were strumming out a dramatic song as I arrived.

The restaurant is right on Queen Street, with large plate glass windows letting in a nice view of the pedestrians passing by who stop and stare in to watch the show.

I stopped where the maître d was standing to greet me when I saw Stella waving from a table. I moved between the occupied tables and made my way over to her. God she was pretty, dangerously pretty.

"How was your trip?" I asked, as I neared the table.

"It was a bunch of meetings and a hotel room, followed by a delay at the airport."

I pulled my chair out and sat down. "You haven't ordered yet," I noted.

"I was waiting for you."

"Well, thank you."

"By the way, I like the music," she said.

"Oh yes, this place is great. I come hear about once a month. Do you like Flamenco?"

"I do. I don't really listen to it regularly, but the guitar work is unlike any other kind of music." She sat and stared at the gentleman who was playing, watching his fingers as they moved rapidly and with precision up and down the strings.

A waitress stepped up to the table wearing a black skirt and bright white shirt. She was probably thirty, thin and with a pleasant smile. She handed us the menus and wine list.

"Hi, my name is Gabriella and I'll be your hostess for the evening. Here is the wine and beer menu. Would you like to start with some drinks?"

I looked at Stella. She looked at me.

"Do you like Spanish wines?" I asked.

"I do."

I turned to Gabriella. "Could you give us a moment to ruminate on this?"

Gabriella smiled and spun on her heel to go check on another table. She had a long ponytail in back which was thick and braided and swung way out as she spun around. I thought how pretty it would look if she was performing Flamenco.

Stella and I talked wines for the next fifteen minutes. We got totally distracted as we discussed the differing virtues of wine regions in Spain, and then the characteristics of the different wines themselves. Stella's eyes sparkled as we talked. The green eyes across the table from me were enchanting. I could see why Jonathan could have become obsessed with her.

Since we both primarily wanted Tapas with seafood we agreed to order a nice Albarino.

We continued to talk about wine while Gabriella brought it out and poured us each a glass. I breathed in the aromas of Clementines and apricots. Before taking a sip I extended my glass toward Stella and said, "Santé." Stella touched her glass to mine and replied, "Santé." We each took a sip. It was crisp and distinctive, strongly acidic, and complex but smooth. It made me think of Isabelle.

After ordering we sat and listened to the music and watched the dancer spin and stomp her heels in her brightly colored dress. I needed to talk to Stella about the case, but wining and dining a suspect, if you can tolerate the person's company, is one of the easiest ways to get them to let down their hair. You can usually gain far more information with a good meal and relaxing ambiance than you can ever gain by simply knocking on a door and standing with a notepad in your hand as you record every word they are saying.

I waited until we were well into our tapas. Then, as I was about to broach the subject Stella's curiosity couldn't be contained any longer and she asked, "Frank, this is a wonderful dinner and exceptional wine, but, did you actually ask me out to talk about the stolen files or something else?"

"I do need to ask you some things about the case. Jonathan is paying for all of this and to be honest, it's much more pleasant to talk over a good meal and a glass of wine."

"You are very smooth Frank, you know that?"

I smiled and said, "I try." I lifted my wine glass and she lifted hers and touched it to mine.

"So how is your investigation going? Did you recover the briefcase?"

"Not yet. Whoever took it is brilliant."

She stared at me with a blank expression.

"Jonathan thinks you're behind it," I said.

She furrowed her eyebrows and looked puzzled.

"You look surprised," I noted.

"I'm shocked. I'm confounded, bewildered."

"Good adjectives," I noted.

She looked at me. "Why in the world would he think that?"

"To be honest, that's what I wanted to ask you. Technically, someone with your past history with Jonathan and SPURRIER AND FREEN would certainly have motive. But what's curious to me is that he would think you would use a hooker to steal the briefcase and would resort to something like this as a vendetta. Is there any reason he would be justified in thinking that?"

"Oh my god. I, I can't believe he would think something like that of me. I mean, do you honestly think I would do something like that?"

"No, and Ted Freen doesn't think you

would either. But I was hoping you could shed some light on why Jonathan might be so convinced. Stella, I hate to ask this question, but I need to. Was there ever anything more between you and Jonathan than what you told me before?"

"Do you think I lied to you Frank?"

"Stella, it's not that I don't believe you, but Jonathan seems very convinced you are the major suspect. I need to know why he feels so strongly about that."

"I haven't so much as talked to the man in a year and a half."

"Do you and Ted Freen talk or e-mail about company business?"

"Of course. Ted asks me questions to pick my brain. That's how I know their research has come to a grinding halt."

"Do you think Ted shares things you tell him with Jonathan?"

"He might. I don't know."

"Ted is a minion. My guess is he shares everything with Jonathan. Do you recall ever saying anything at all, even in jest, about taking their data, or wishing Jonathan's company might be ruined?"

She looked flustered and upset. "Um, I don't know. I probably have. Ted and I are friends and we talk about Jonathan. God, am I going to be implicated in this?"

"Jonathan could try to. Is it at all possible

Ted might have misconstrued your comments and told Jonathan about it as if he was concerned?"

"God, I don't think so. Oh my god, I might be implicated in all of this."

I took a sip of wine and tried to give her some space. Stella looked panicked, someone who's never been in trouble in her life, suddenly imagining themselves being arrested and losing everything. I've seen this reaction many times before.

As we sat there the guitar player was doing a fast picking part of a song, alternating thumping the guitar with lightning fast finger movement. The Flamenco dancer spun and flipped her legs back, punctuating the music with her large movements. Stella glanced over at the guitar player, her eyes looked sad. She lived in her sheltered world of research and science. She suddenly turned her eyes on me.

"Frank, you believe me don't you?"

"I do believe you Stella. Listen, I didn't bring you here to put you on the spot. I just wanted to pick your brain to get a sense of why Jonathan might believe this so strongly."

"But what am I going to do if he accuses me?" She looked really worried.

"Stella, I am the one investigating this. The police aren't even involved at this point."

"And you really don't think I did it?"

"No, you didn't do it. And I will catch

the people who did, make no mistake about it."

"And you really don't think I did it?"

"I know you didn't do it."

She looked back and forth between my eyes to see if I was telling the truth. Her face relaxed slightly. "So was there anything else?"

"No, you told me exactly what I needed to hear."

"So, you really, truly believe me that I had nothing to do with the stolen data?"

"I truly believe that, yes."

She let out an expulsion of air, "Whew, god, look Frank, to be honest, my nerves are shot. I need to get out of here."

I thanked her. She took off. I sat and listened to the music and ordered a good bottle of one of their Rioja wines. This was all going on Jonathan's bill anyway. The wine was potent and strong. As the dancer and guitar player continued I pulled out a notepad and jotted down what Stella had said. Jonathan was no fool. Why did he feel so strongly that Stella was involved?

Chapter 31

I woke up thinking of Isabelle. Shit. I thought of the other night, the love making, the long bath eating shrimp and her falling asleep with her head in my lap. She was the most beguiling woman I have ever known, strong and smart, so sexy that I was powerless at times just looking at her. Yet she had moments when she was so soft and tender and almost innocent in her trust. She was complex.

I went downstairs. Fiona was sitting at the bar, reading the paper and drinking a cup of coffee. It was only 9:30 and the place was still locked up tight. Fiona looked up as I entered.

"Mornin' Frank. There's coffee in the kitchen."

"Hm," I uttered.

A moment later I slid up on a stool at the bar beside her with a steaming mug in my hand. I sat staring at it quietly while Fiona read the paper. After a moment she turned her head and looked at me. That flaming red hair of hers was always floating around her face like a fiery picture frame.

"Clinic's open if you wanna talk," she stated.

I smiled slightly and looked at her. "Damn you and that Irish woman's intuition."

"Is it lady trouble?" She asked.

I narrowed my eyes and stared at her. "How the hell do you do that?"

"I've been a bartender one hell of a long time Frank. Plus, you don't tend to be morose or somber except when it comes to women."

"Really? Is that true?"

"Yep."

"Shit."

"Is it Isabelle or someone else?"

"Isabelle."

"So what's the problem Frank? You too seem like you are utterly infatuated with each other after all this time. Do you know how rare that is?"

"I guess."

"Then what's the problem?"

I laughed lightly and took a sip of coffee. "You do cut through all the bullshit don't you?"

"Hey, I deal with drunks and assholes all

day long. What can I say?"

I took another sip of coffee.

"Do you think I'm just like every other guy?"

"Do you mean do I think you tend to have a one track mind, think primarily about yourself, put your needs above the needs of everyone else around you, have a hard time talking about anything other than alcohol, sports, cars and guns, and get turned on every time a warm body walks into a room that is emitting female pheromones?"

"Damn you."

"Hey Frank, honestly, you are a manly man, but, to answer your question, no, you my friend are not like any other guy. The other night, after you cleaned the floor with those guys who were going to rob me, you didn't come in here the next day and brag and beat your chest about it like a great ape trying to show everyone you are dominant. That's what most guys would have done. And when you're girlfriend called all worried about you, most guys would have acted all macho and told their story as if they were a conquering cave man. You just played it all down and tried to make her feel better."

"Well, I didn't want her to worry."

"I know Frank. That's exactly my point. You aren't like most guys."

I stared down at my coffee and took

another sip.

"Seriously Frank, how come you and Isabelle go for long periods without seeing one another? And you dance around each other sometimes while at the same time it is obvious you two are crazy about each other?"

"We're so much alike. We have both seen the worst side of people too many times. We're both serious workaholics. I drove my ex-wife away because of my work. As much as I like Isa I'm sure if we were together too much I would do the same to her. I think she feels the same way. So when we get too close we both vanish for a while. I guess it's to make sure we don't get any closer."

Fiona has the bartender shrink thing down to a science. She asks questions and then really listens.

"What you're saying is you actually like her too much."

"No, I mean, well, shit, I don't know."

"Do you love her Frank?"

I took another sip of coffee and didn't answer.

Fiona looked at me. "Well let me tell you something my dysfunctional friend, that woman loves you."

"I don't kno…………"

"No Frank, I'm telling you point blank. I've seen it in her eyes. Some nights when you two are in the bar I've seen Mitch and other guys hit on her while you're in the bathroom, and all she does is keep staring at the bathroom door waiting for you. Then her eyes light up when you walk out of that bathroom."

I smiled. Staring down into my coffee I said, "You know Isa and I can talk for hours, or we can sit for hours and saying nothing at all," I said, as much to myself as to Fiona.

"Well, don't wait too long my friend. That is one beautiful woman and no woman will wait forever."

"I don't know Fiona. I don't even really understand what the hell is going on between us."

"Do you want to go out with any other women?"

"No."

"Does she ever go out with any other men?"

"No."

"Well, maybe you just shouldn't worry about it then. Maybe just enjoy it for whatever the hell it is. But make no mistake it about Frank, that woman is crazy as hell about you. She's got it bad."

We both sipped our coffee.

"You ever get lonely Fiona?"

She took a sip of her coffee and set the mug down on the bar, "I guess. Most of the time I'm too busy to think about it."

I laughed. "I know, me too. We're both

pathetic, you know that?"

She laughed. She held her mug up and I touched mine to it. We both took a sip.

"We're both workaholics Frank. Mitch is an alcoholic, you and me are workaholics. They're both addictions. You and I just do something more productive with ours."

"Productive addicts, hey, well, it could be worse."

"I will say Frank, Isabelle is one of the prettiest women I have ever seen. Her eyes are intense aren't they?"

"I know. God her eyes are so gorgeous that sometimes when we are talking I lose track of what I'm thinking because I get so lost staring into her eyes."

"What does she drink? Is she one of those martini ladies, a fruity drink person or whiskey drinker?"

"She loves wine."

Fiona turned and stared at me. "Well there you go. How much better does it get than that? Sheesh, I should charge double for this session."

Fiona and I drank another cup and chatted lightly. Then I went up and pulled on my good jeans and leather jacket and went out to deal with what I needed to do.

Chapter 32

I headed over to Dean and Delucca's on M Street, got a pastry and another steaming hot black coffee. I sat outside. It was chilly but it felt good to breathe in the air and think. As I sipped my coffee I started making phone calls.

I started with Dogbone to see if there were any updates. Petra still seemed to be okay, or at least living and breathing. She never called me back, but she was a street person, I figured she wouldn't. At least she was okay. There had been no more phone calls between Dex and Jonathan or Lily. Charlotte's phone was still at the address where Dogbone had tracked it to. She was either laying low until this blew over or she had ditched the phone. I had Angel over watching the house and he hadn't seen any signs of life. No one had come in or out since he had been there.

There was really nothing turning up on background info or on suspicious phone calls from Reggie or Nancy. And since we had a person who was asking for a ransom it seemed like corporate spying was out of the picture, unless there was more to it and the perpetrator was going to stiff Jonathan and Ted and then turn around and sell it to someone else.

I clearly was missing something. My mind kept rehashing the same possible scenarios and rerunning the same lists of evidence I had. It was like watching reruns of some old sitcom over and over again in my head, where you've heard the lines repeated too many times and the jokes and lines all start to blur together so that you really don't hear them anymore.

In theory, Jonathan and Ted were going to be getting the briefcase back, which was really all they wanted. Also, the fact that nothing suspicious was turning up on the credit cards from Jonathan's wallet all made it seem like things were what they seemed on the surface, a robbery and a ransom. But how the hell could this be so neat and clean? A hooker had been recruited and then she vanished along with the briefcase. Everything seemed to keep pointing back to Charlotte and the strange relationship between Lily and Dex. There was a part of me that almost hoped it was Lily and that she got away with it. She deserved some happiness, but hell, she wasn't the one paying my bill.

We never resolved anything with Reggie and his embassy friend. I sat thinking about it and wondered if the Chinese consulate ever used Dex's escort services to entertain diplomats. What if Dex's ladies had been employed by them and through that Charlotte had been recruited by them. Reggie might well have known about the escort service, maybe even about Charlotte. I called Dogbone back.

"Hey Dogbreath."

"What do you need Frankie?"

"Has there been anything new at all with Reggie Tsui's friend at the embassy?"

"I still can't crack into his phone."

"Have you run a detailed check on this guy through your contacts at the various acronyms you work for?"

"I have. His name is Cheng Lee. He is former Chinese military, now working for the embassy. One of my buddies says Cheng works for The Ministry of State Security, has a nice little corner office in Beijing, but has been stationed here for the last two years."

"Damn, nice work Dogbone. Do your sources have him pegged for any espionage in this country?"

"He's suspected on numerous things. But he's Teflon, nothing sticks."

"How about old Reggie?"

"Hold on Frank, if Cheng and Reggie did steal it for the mother land in the Far East, why would they be asking for a ransom?"

"Who knows Dogbone? They might be using this to delay things while they work on getting the information out of the country. Or maybe they already got the info out of the country and this is their way of covering their tracks so there is no suspicion of espionage. If it looks like a simple theft it keeps all eyes off of China."

"Damn, you're good Frank."

"I just like to consider all possibilities. Do you know where Cheng lives?"

"I'm insulted. What kind of a question is that?"

I laughed. "Give me his damn address."

I wrote it down. He lived across the river in Rosslyn. He was married with no kids. I wondered if his wife was a cover. Dogbone said he would e-mail a photo of Cheng.

This whole investigation was on such a narrow timeframe now because of the ransom. I decided that since Charlotte was not moving I would pull Angel and get him to stake out Cheng. Since he was Chinese Intelligence he might be a tough one to tail, and if he was really involved then he would likely know who I was and that I was investigating the missing documents. He likely wouldn't know about Angel, so it made sense to let Angel cover him.

Angel sounded relieved when I told him to change over to watching Cheng. Shit, I wasn't used to an investigation being on quite this kind of time frame. With homicides some can take a long time. Others can be time sensitive, like if the murder is suspected of being connected to a serial killing. Then you know you need to work fast and continuously. But this whole case had unfolded in a matter of days and the list of suspects wasn't getting any shorter.

I figured my own best bet might be to interview Reggie again. I tried calling him several times but he didn't answer. He might be ignoring my calls after our last talk.

Then Angel called.

"Hey Frank, Reggie just went in Cheng's house."

"Was he carrying anything?"

"A backpack and his headphones."

I paused to think.

"You there Frank?"

"Yeah, yeah, okay, when Reggie comes out see what he is carrying. Follow him to wherever he goes."

"What about Cheng?"

"I say stay with Reggie for now. He sounds like he goes out a lot at night to party. Hang out at his place. If it looks like he is going out for the evening then burgle his home and see what you can find."

"Is there anything in particular I am

looking for?"

"I wish there was. No, just look for any notes he has written about people he is meeting with, plans, etc. If he has a laptop then go ahead and steal it and we'll let Dogbone go through it. And try to find that backpack he wore into Cheng's and go through it with a fine tooth comb."

"Got it boss."

We disconnected.

I headed back to Fiona's for lunch. I ordered a big bowl of chili with fresh onions and a mound of cheese on top. I sat eating it as I tried to relax my mind.

The chili was spicy, hot and rich with meat and tomato sauce. There was a big pile of red onions and shredded cheddar on top. Fiona adds beer and molasses to it to for flavor and to thicken it and add body. I spooned it into my mouth slowly, chased it with a Beck's and stared out the window at people walking by on M Street.

How the hell was Reggie, Dex and Lily involved in all of this? Lily seemed like such a lush who was resigned to where she was, content to surround herself with wealth and money and keep her blood alcohol level high enough to let all the crap around her roll right off. But, she was in love with Charlotte, on some level. She was also jilted, repeatedly. Love and being screwed over by a lover are powerful motives.

My mind was wandering aimlessly. I ate slowly and let my thoughts bounce around from one place to another like a little pinball bouncing off the little bumper paddles and obstacles, randomly knocking it about from one wall to the other.

Chapter 33

It was already early evening and I felt like I had wasted the day, spinning my wheels and not getting anywhere. It was beginning to rain again outside. I went up to my apartment and grabbed my raincoat. I took a long walk through Georgetown. It was chilly. The light misty rain was making the streets and windshields of passing cars glisten as they reflected the lights of the city. I passed couples and groups of people bundled up, having private conversations and laughing as they passed by. I thought of Isabelle and wondered what she was doing.

I couldn't focus my thoughts on where to go with all of the new twists in the case. Time was running out. We would meet with the perps tomorrow. Money would be wired. The briefcase might or might not be returned and I would get paid. But it would be such an unsatisfying paycheck if all I did was spin my wheels this whole time. For me, it wasn't about helping my client. He was a piece of shit. I just hate to do a half-assed job on anything and I really hate to be duped. I fucking can't stand to be duped.

I walked to the far end of M Street to where Key Bridge enters D.C., dumping all the traffic from Virginia directly into Georgetown, like a main artery dumping a constant flow of blood into the heart. I waited for an opening and darted across between cars. Two people honked their horns at me. I made it to the double yellow line, waited there while another person honked and dashed the remainder of the way across. I passed a row of two story buildings and store fronts and then walked past Dixie Liquor. I paused to stare in the window. It's one of those liquor stores that everyone on both sides of the river know about and make pilgrimages to for all their party supplies.

I walked past Dixie and the parking lot and rounded the corner where the very steep Exorcist steps are located between buildings. It was dark and eerily lit up by the orange glow of street lamps. I started climbing the stairs and with the mist falling around me I couldn't help but to think of the movie. These steps are famous in Georgetown and people still climb them and talk about the movie after all these decades. I passed two groups of Georgetown University students on the stairs, heading off to some nighttime destination.

At the top of the stairs I continued on toward the Georgetown Campus. The large stone walls, iron fence and tall stony spires of the campus loomed up in the misty night. It always seems European to me with its magnificent towers and tall stony structures. It sits high above the Potomac and the Washington skyline, as if the lofty thoughts of the institution somehow rise above the pettiness of the politics in Washington. The large iron fence and walls seem to protect it and maintain the ambiance of a place where thoughts and ideals are still protected and honored. I frequently walk here when I need to lift my thoughts and clear my head.

The damp night air was working its magic and I knew what I needed to do, even though I hated to do it. I stepped under the green awning of a small corner market, out of the weather. I pulled out my cell phone and called Jonathan.

"Jonathan?"

"Frank? It's late. I was just climbing into bed. Is everything okay?"

"I have some very interesting twists in all of this."

"Like what?"

I took a deep breath and stared out at the rain, collecting my thoughts.

"First off, I found Charlotte."

"You found her? How did you find her? Have you talked to her? Is she involved in the exchange part of this? Was she able to tell you anything about who did this?"

"No, no, I have nothing other than where she is."

"Well can't you arrest her? Can't you, I don't know, take her into custody? I mean, we might be able to nail these bastards before I have to pay them." He spoke with great excitement.

"Your uh, your wife Lily knows where she is." I said it with hesitation. I liked Lily. I felt sorry for her being attached to this bastard. But the truth was the truth and he was paying my bills, not her.

There was a pause. "Lily knows where she is?"

"Jonathan, is there any possibility that Lily could be involved in this?"

"Lily, shit, how fucking stupid of me. My little inebriated, art loving spouse. God….." His voice trailed off.

I gave him a minute. The rain was starting to come down harder. I tucked my other hand down into my coat pocket and pulled the polar fleece collar up about my neck and ears.

"You sure?" Jonathan asked.

"Yeah, I'm sure."

"God, how could I have been so stupid?"

"The question is whether she is just in it with Charlotte, or is someone else in it with them?"

I could hear him putting ice into a glass and the gurgling sound of him pouring a drink. He took a loud sip and swallowed.

"You know Frank, my wife has just slipped into an almost torpid state of existence. She is usually drunk by the time I get home at night." I heard him take another sip. "But, she is a brilliant woman. And, well, I know she loves Charlotte. Lily and I slept with Charlotte together, you know, like, well, anyway, I think you get the picture. Afterward Lily seemed smitten by her and said I was an asshole for exploiting her. She seemed to take on some kind of bullshit notion of being her protector. I don't know, saving her or something."

"What connection is there between Lily and Dex?"

He took another sip. "Well, I use him to set up girls for parties I throw for politicians and people coming into town on business trips. Lily sometimes calls for me."

"Well apparently Dex and Lily have talked and even met up privately numerous times. I imagine it's possible that he and Charlotte and Lily could be in on this together."

"Well Lily has the brains and I know she has at least one Grand Cayman account where she socks away money that I allow her to have."

There was a long pause. I heard him take a long sip and then pour more liquid into the glass.

"That bitch," he mumbled. "That fucking bitch."

"It's your money, what do you want to do?" I asked.

"Well, Lily surely knows all of my business associates and my competition. It's not hard to imagine that she would sell it in a heartbeat to one of them just for the pure satisfaction of ruining me."

I had no problem understanding how or why Lily would do that. In truth, I wouldn't blame her.

"Shit! Damn that little devious bitch!"

"Well, what do you want to do?"

"I don't think we have any choice. I just didn't think she was sober enough to even attempt something like this."

"Jealousy and being jilted can be very sobering and a powerful motivator."

"Well, I'm glad you called anyway Frank because I received another anonymous note today and they said they wanted you to accompany me to make the exchange."

"When did this happen?" I asked.

"I just received it about an hour ago. The

note was attached to my car when I went to pick it up at the parking garage."

"Did it say why they want me to come with you?"

"Well, wait, let me get the note and read it to you," Jonathan said. I heard him set his glass down and get up. A heard paper rustling. Then he started to speak. "It says, *Jonathan, it has come to my attention that you have a private investigator employed, a retired cop. That was not very nice of you. You bring him with you to make the exchange, where I can keep an eye on him. There are to be no guns or weapons of any kind. I will have back-up with me and if anything goes wrong I will deal with the both of you and the briefcase goes to the highest bidder.*"

"Interesting, well, I did interrogate Dex rather vigorously," I noted.

"Can you meet me at SPURRIER AND FREEN tomorrow morning, about a half hour before the exchange?"

"Yeah, sure."

"Frank, I'm sure it's against your nature, but they did say no guns or weapons."

"Yeah, well, I gotta think about that."

"You think they would try something?"

"I don't know about Lily or Charlotte, but Dex would."

"I doubt he's stupid enough to kill an ex-cop."

"Hm, maybe."

"Look Frank, I can't afford to lose $50 million dollars and my company. How about we meet in Ted's office before they get there. Then, we can hide your gun in the office somewhere so that if they search you they'll think you're unarmed. Then you can stand near it throughout the transaction and be ready to draw it just in case."

It wasn't a bad idea. "That could work."

"Look Frank. I know you don't like me. And I imagine you are doing this primarily for Dani and for the money. But, I know you are someone who gets the job done. That's what Dani told me. Once we get the briefcase back you will be generously reimbursed for your trouble."

"Alright Jonathan, well, I will see you tomorrow morning."

"Okay, and remember, be there about a half hour before the scheduled time so we have time to hide your gun and also in case traffic or anything delays us."

"Alright, one half hour before the arranged time."

We disconnected. I stood under the awning watching the rain fall and staring out at the night. After a while I pulled my collar up and stepped out into the wetness. I needed to think some more. I felt off my game and unsteady. It wouldn't be the first time I had either underestimated or overlooked suspects. It happens, particularly in cases where there is virtually no tangible evidence to go on.

At one point I stepped back under an awning and called Angel. He had burgled Reggie's apartment and had come up empty handed. I disconnected with him and stepped back out into the rain.

I walked on through the night. I couldn't relax. My mind was racing. I walked up one street and down another. I got soaked to the bone but walked on. The more tired I got the more my mental chatter calmed down and I started to see connections, pieces of the jigsaw puzzle. Sometimes when you are working on a big puzzle you stare it for an hour without being able to fit a single piece into place and then at some point you finally find one that fits and suddenly you see where a whole bunch of other pieces fit as well. Charlotte, Dex and Lily, why the hell hadn't I seen the roles they had played in this earlier? Things were beginning to make sense.

When I got back to my apartment I was shivering on the outside but I finally had a handle on what I believed had happened. Pieces were beginning to fit together and I could see the connections.

I took a hot shower and stood under it a long time to warm myself up. At least now that I had a handle on it I felt at least I could go into it with eyes wide open. No matter what happened, at least now it all made sense and I knew exactly what I had to do.

Chapter 34

I only caught a couple of hours of sleep and was up long before my alarm. I went downstairs to the bar and had coffee. Fiona offered to make me some eggs, but I couldn't eat. I got on the road early to head out toward Chantilly. I was going against traffic, but I-66 can be a mess any time of the day. It took me an hour and fifteen minutes to get out there.

When I arrived I saw Jonathan's car in the parking lot. I went into the office reception area and pushed the buzzer. Jonathan came out and we walked back to Ted's office. He looked amazingly calm.

When we got to Ted's office Jonathan asked me if I wanted a drink. I told him I was good. He reached under the desk and pulled out one glass for himself and a bottle of Vodka. He popped the top on a can of Orangina and mixed the two. He took a sip and then turned and looked out the window. It was cloudy outside and chilly.

"So are you ready?" I asked him.

"I guess as ready as I'll ever be." He looked at his watch, took another sip and then turned around to face me. "I guess we should get ready. Can I have your gun? I was thinking I would put it here in the desk drawer. You can stand over here by the drawer and be ready to grab it."

"Makes sense," I replied.

I reached around behind me and pulled out my Sig. I flipped it around and held it by the barrel, offering him the handle. He took it from me and set it in the drawer. He paused a moment and took a sip of his drink. He looked at me and then lifted a .45 Colt Commander out of the same drawer and pointed it at my chest.

"Well Frank, now we really are ready."

I stared into his eyes.

"Oh, this?" He asked, holding the gun up slightly for me to get a better look at it. "Ahh yes, well you see Frank, things aren't exactly what they appear to be."

He moved around the desk and waved the gun, motioning for me to move in front of the window. I did as he asked.

"I hate having my back to a window, you

know? I like to know what's behind me. You never can trust people." He said it with that smug grin of his, which I felt like smacking off his face.

"So you played everybody didn't you? You have people who sing your praises and practically worship you. And all the while you're playing both sides of the fence. You fit right in here in Washington. You should have been a politician."

He smiled. "Why thank you Frank."

"I have to say your little act of looking so pathetic and distraught when I first met with you was good."

"You just figured it out? You are very astute Frank."

"No, actually I became suspicious of it after I talked with Lily and then the clerks at the hotel. Lily said you never get distraught or upset about anything. I watched you after that and she was right, you never get upset about anything. Then the clerks told me about Charlotte leaving through the hotel lobby and setting the briefcase down and drawing attention to herself where everyone could see her with it. It corroborated your story but it was a little too neat and tidy. Most thieves are street smart and would never leave through a hotel lobby and draw attention to themselves like that."

"Well, I needed to make it clear that I had

nothing to do with it. You have to admit, Charlotte played her role very well."

"Well, it seemed a bit too perfect. But, I do applaud you for that. I was suspicious, but you did a nice job covering up your tracks. You almost fooled me, up until last night. That was when you made your first big slip up."

"And just what was that?"

"It was when I called last night and told you everything and then out of the blue you thought up to add that you had received another note and I needed to be here too."

"Oh, I don't know, it worked didn't it?"

"Almost."

He chuckled. "Well considering where I am standing and where you are standing, I would say it worked quite well."

"I am always suspicious of coincidences Jonathan. I walked a long time last night after we hung up and finally put all the pieces together. It struck me about the timing of you adding this new little twist because when I called you last night you stated that it was late and you were about ready to go to bed. Then, after I told you about finding Charlotte you added that you were just about to call me."

He smiled slightly, seeming amused.

"That's when I remembered something Ted told me. He said you are the kind of man who someone should never play chicken with. He said you would die rather than lose. That's when the pieces starting falling into place. You're company is going under. Stella told me your research has gone nowhere. Robert Petrucelli confirmed that. And it has been bugging me, why would someone want to steal something that many people know is going under? And, more importantly, since you obviously know it is going under, why would you pay $50 million dollars to get it back?"

Jonathan's smile broadened. "Go on."

"If your company goes under then you lose, and you would rather die than lose. So you've just kept everybody believing in you while you began stealing them blind."

"I've always had a gift for making people believe in me." He smiled. "Well, I applaud your marvelous detective work. It's true our research has been stagnant for some time. Ted is so loyal he will go down with the ship and his loyalty and steadfastness will buoy him up. He has enough in the bank to retire comfortably to his boat in Italy."

"Well, that was magnanimous of you to insist that he not put in any of his own money," I said.

"Yes, it was, wasn't it? But you know Frank, Ted's the kind of guy who never really had vision. He knew we were floundering but he's like a dog, faithful to the end. He believed in our company because he trusts me." He laughed. "He's too naïve and trusting to be a good business man. He never really learned to play hardball with the big boys, you know? He was too much of a follower."

I stared at him. He had the look on his face of someone who is very satisfied with himself.

"You obviously didn't ask me to come here just so you could tell me all of this. So, I surmise you decided to make sure I don't come after you."

"It wasn't originally in my plan Frank, but you are a lot better than I thought you were. And after what you did to Dex the other night everyone will believe he had the perfect motive to kill you. It's all simple arithmetic. You're too dangerous to keep around and I have the perfect person to frame for it."

"So where are you going to disappear to Jonathan, let's see, is it the Caribbean? I've read you spend a lot of time down there.

"Is my plan really that transparent Frank?" He laughed out loud. "You are truly a marvelous detective. Yes, that is exactly what I am going to do. Yes, soon, poor Jonathan Spurrier will be murdered and leave this world forever, and be born again under a new alias in his own little paradise. You know Frank, I have to confess you have figured out far more than I ever gave you credit for."

"Oh, I've had hypothesizes I have been developing all along. It was the phone call last night that confirmed which one was correct."

"Well you have been a naughty employee Frank and as your employer I have to say I should fire you for not keeping me more up to date on the developments in this case." He laughed out loud at his own cleverness.

"People like you are why I never share my theories during a case, with anyone."

He stood patiently listening with a smile on his face like a proud artist admiring his handiwork.

"The way you made all of the evidence point toward Lily and Dex was clever. Using Lily's phone with text messages to Dex, so anyone later reading them would think they had been plotting all along. It was clever, not terribly original, but clever."

"Yes, my darlin'g wife. I have to admit, I was pretty pleased with myself over that one. I told her where I was keeping Charlotte. I told her I was keeping her there for her own good, her own protection. Of course Lily wanted to go see her, which made her seem even more involved. I used Lily's phone all the time for calls to Dex and Charlotte, etc, so if anyone was tapping my phone they would see that Lily was the one doing it all. You see Frank since Charlotte is about to vanish with me all the evidence will point to my darlin'g wife and Dex."

"Yes, the police can see the phone calls

and text messages between them. That was smart."

"I thought so too." He took another sip of his drink and set the glass down on the desk.

"So you are going to implicate Dex and Lily together on this."

"It won't be hard for anyone to believe. She has loathed me for years."

"And Dex, I imagine it didn't take a lot to convince him that you would pay him far more than he could ever hope to make off the street if he went along helping you steal it. He just didn't know he was going to be left behind."

"Very good Frank, Dex had to be brought in because he has the kind of criminal record that makes him easy to incriminate and Charlotte was too afraid of him to help me on her own. He ended up being an important player in all of this. "

"One of your pawns?"

"Perhaps more like a bishop, as he was a little more of a key player in all of this."

"Just for my own edification, I assume that you put so much focus on Stella because she was so clean you figured it would keep a little more distance, keep me busy."

"I needed to do something to slow you down Frank. You are quite good."

"And I am hypothesizing that the little cameo role I played in all of this was to make it look like you were trying everything in your power to get the documents back, hiring a topnotch P.I., diverting suspicion away from you."

He smiled, "Your hypothesis is correct. I had to make it look like I was doing everything in my power to catch the wascally wabbit who was blackmailing my company. I needed a P.I. Dani said you are the best. I thought it would be fun to match wits with the great detective. I figured it would be a great chess match."

"Pawns, bishops, queens, all the chess pieces, that's how you see everyone. They're all just sacrificial pieces in your little game."

"Some are pawns, a few are bishops or knights. The only piece you can't sacrifice in a game Frank is the King. When he is lost the game is over."

"You're not a king Jonathan. That's where chess and real life don't overlap. Everyone is just a pawn. Everyone is expendable. When you've seen enough dead bodies in your lifetime, seen them laying there, knowing that no matter who or what they were before, the world will just go on without them now, filling their shoes with someone else. Then you realize there are no bishops or knights or rooks. It's only on a chess board Jonathan that the game ends with a king being taken. In real life they just get replaced by another king or some other despot. As for you and you're company? If it goes under the game doesn't stop. Robert Petrucelli or a dozen other companies just step in to take your place. You think way too much of yourself Jonathan, you're just an overdressed pawn."

"As you like Frank, but, for the record, I will be a very wealthy pawn. And on my private island in the Carribean, I will be king."

"I suppose down there you won't be a pawn, maybe more like a prawn."

Jonathan smiled slightly, "Hm, yes, prawn, shrimp, Carribean, very clever."

"I try."

There was an awkward pause.

"You know Jonathan, as of right now you still haven't purloined your company's funds. If you stop right now and hand me that gun I'm certain with a good lawyer you could minimize the charges and maybe not even do any jail time."

"You really don't get it do you Frank?"

I studied his face. "Hm," I chuckled slightly. "Yes, actually I do Jonathan. Ted was right, you would rather die than lose."

"I never lose Frank. No, like I said before, I didn't figure I would have to kill you. But you were far better than I anticipated. Please don't take it personally Frank. It's just business and you got in the way."

"Hm, just business? I'll keep that in mind. And how about Lily? You'll sacrifice Lily so you can go live in luxury somewhere humping your little girlfriend?" As I asked I took a step left, moving away from the window, toward the edge of the desk. I needed to get into a better position, so I continued to engage him. "So, humor me, out of professional curiosity, how are you even going to implicate Dex in this?"

"Dex will be here shortly. I asked him to show up to meet me here so I can pay him. With his payoff I will also have stashed the gun into the bottom of his bag, under the money, after I have shot you of course. Then he will simply leave, but people will see that he was here. And the murder weapon will be in his possession. On Monday they'll find your body in here. They'll also find some of my blood, which I will extract with a hypodermic needle and pour it on the floor. I'll add a tuft of pulled hair to go with it just for good measure. I'll add a few drops of blood and hair to the inside of his car for good measure. Of course I will have disappeared off the face of the earth, and they will assume that Dex disposed of me somewhere. "

There was a long pause. Jonathan looked at his watch. I took another small step left. I tried to judge Jonathan's angle from me around the desk.

"You know Frank, I have to confess, I'm glad at least you lived up to the hype. You made the game a little more challenging. I would like to congratulate Dani on recommending you, but

I guess I will have to refrain." He chuckled.

"You are a very smart man Jonathan. I'll give you that."

"That's very big of you," he said. He looked down at his watch again and I took another small step left.

"Well, Frank, if you'll excuse me I do have a phone call to make, money to transfer and a plane to catch. So, as you see I have a pretty busy schedule."

I took another slight step to the left and started raising my hands. Jonathan smiled at seeing me show a sign of surrender.

"It's a little late for that Frank. You needn't bother putting your hands up."

I continued to raise them and took one more step left around the desk.

Jonathan narrowed his eyes at me suspiciously. "What are you going to do, make a play for me Frank?" He shook his head back and forth.

"Put your hands down," he stated.

I continued to raise them. I could see his mind working, wondering what was going on. I could see the chess player pondering if all of his pieces were covered, wondering if he had missed something. He looked suspiciously around the room. Then he looked toward the window behind me, right as the glass shattered. I felt glass rain down on my head and back as the bullet hit his face dead center. I saw

Jonathan's head explode like a watermelon smashed with a sledge hammer, pieces flying out and falling to the ground. His body was thrown backward like a ragdoll tossed violently onto the floor.

I felt shards of glass in my hair as I lifted my head up and looked at the lifeless heap on the floor in front of me. I took a deep breath and stepped toward his crumpled body. As I moved toward him I suddenly heard the crackly voice of my guardian angel in my ear? "You alright boss man?"

"Nice shootin' Angel."

"Thanks, you alright?"

"Yeah, but what the hell were you waiting for? I told you when I started raising my hands to shoot the prick."

"Ah, you were alright. I had him in my scope the whole time. I was just enjoying listening to your little synopsis you were giving him."

"You damn lunkhead," I mumbled.

"Are you alright?" Angel asked.

I looked down at my shoes and replied, "Well, I have Jonathan goo all over my damn shoes. I liked these shoes damn it."

"Well you should have stayed back a little farther. I was using my .50 caliber rifle to make sure the thick glass wouldn't cause any variation in the shot."

I stared down at the crumpled mass that

was Jonathan. "Well, I would say there was definitely no variation in your shot." Then I asked, "Hey Dogbone, did you get it all on tape?"

"I don't use tape Frank. It's all digital."

"Whatever, did you get the confession?"

"I did. It's good stuff."

"Glad you're pleased. Go ahead and call 911. Tell them I am here waiting for them. Then go pick up Charlotte."

"10-4, I'm on the way."

"Hey Angel?"

"Yeah?"

"You pick up Dex when he arrives."

"My pleasure. Do you care what kind of condition he's in when we turn him over?"

I smiled. "We'll tell the police he resisted arrest."

"I was hoping you'd say that." Angel sounded so pleased.

The room was suddenly very quiet. I stepped closer to what had been Jonathan. I squatted down beside his body, resting my elbows on my knees and surveying what was left of him. His handsome face, his arrogance and cocksure attitude were all just a large twisted mass on the floor. I've seen this scene a couple of hundred times before. It's not sick or nasty anymore. It's just my job.

As I studied the body before me, in a soft voice I uttered, "Lies and corruption are nothing new to this town Jonathan. I've been dealing with it for over twenty years and matching wits with people far better than you my friend. Don't take it personally. It's just business." I paused and stared at him a long moment. "By the way, checkmate asshole."

In my ear I heard Angel's voice, "Who you talking to Frank?"

"Just a pawn, a pawn who thought he was a king."

"What?"

"Never mind."

Chapter 35

I stood in front of a bookshelf that went all the way to the ceiling. Shakespeare and Company was packed with people and the narrow spaces between the aisles were barely wide enough to accommodate everyone. I felt like it would only be fitting to pick up something by one of the authors of the Lost Generation while I was shopping at this historic bookshop. I always like Fitzgerald and so I found a nice copy of Tender is the Night. I paid for it and stepped outside. It was starting to rain.

I put my umbrella up and walked down a small side street. Across the Seine and behind some trees I could see the stone spires of Notre Dame Cathedral disappearing into the gray mist.

I waited for the traffic to clear and crossed the Rue Saint Jacques and went to the corner where a café sits at the base of the Hotel Notre Dame. Despite the rain people were crowded beneath the awnings around the little bistro tables. I scanned the huddled masses and saw Isa's dark piercing eyes watching the Parisians as they bustled by on the sidewalks. She suddenly noticed me and her face lit up. Fiona was right.

I pushed my way through the narrow spaces between the tables and leaned over and gave her a kiss on the cheek. Her cheek was cold and I realized I had taken too long in the bookstore.

"You look cold. I'm sorry I took so long," I said.

"I love the smell of Paris in the rain," she said.

"Me too."

She looked at the bag I was holding. "What did you get?"

"I picked up a Scott Fitzgerald book," I said, handing her the bag.

She reached in and pulled out the book along with another one. "What's this one?"

"Oh, it's a present for you. Rimbaud, have you read him?"

"The poet?"

"Not just any poet. He wrote with passion and verve. His writing is raw, twisted, tortured and sad."

"He sounds a lot like you." She smiled. Her eyes sparkled.

I leaned forward and gave her a long soft kiss. I pulled my head back a few inches and stared into her eyes. "You are very astute."

We were interrupted by a handsome middle-aged waiter stepping up to our table.

"Bonjour," he said.

"Bonjour," I replied. "Uh, nous prendons deux cappuccinos, s'il vous plait."

"Oui," he replied and slipped off through the crowd.

I pulled out the chair across from her and sat down. The chill in the damp air went right through my jacket and under my skin, but the sound of the rain drumming on the awning above our heads was soothing. Isa's cheeks were rosy from the chill. It looked good with her eyes.

"So, that was nice of Dani to pay for my trip over with you," she said.

"Well she owed me big time."

"Well, that's not fair. How could she have known that Jonathan was such a low life? Have you talked to Lily to see how she's doing?"

I paused and smiled at Isa.

"What?" She asked.

"You are so beautiful. Your eyes right now are shining like the moon over the ocean at night."

Isa smiled and shook her head at me.

"I'll bet you say that to all the girls."

"Oh," I said, "to get back to your question. Lily is doing great. She is enjoying her new found wealth immensely. And she was delighted when I told her about the private island Jonathan owned under a different name. She is having her lawyers do the paperwork to have it transferred over to her name."

"Is she really going to give you one of her Bogdanoves?"

"She is."

"Frank, you can't accept that. Don't you feel even a little guilty, like you are taking advantage?"

The waiter arrived with our cappuccinos and set them down.

"No, I don't feel guilty. Her husband tried to kill me. She is fabulously wealthy now and hey, if she is grateful and wants to give me a little gift, well, what the hell."

The coffee was strong and hot and fortifying against the cold. We sipped our hot drinks and watched the bustling crowds of Paris shuffling past. There were families and business men and women all mingled in with the younger crowd of men and women dressed in chic clothing, looking like they stepped out of a photo shoot. There was an energy to it all that is just so Paris.

I didn't think about the cases waiting for me back home. I knew there would always be a million other Jonathans out there, runaways, thieves, low life pieces of shit that needed to be tracked down. That could all wait. All I could think about right now was the huge bathtub in Dani's apartment where we were staying, the Musee d'Orsay, walks along the Seine, some good dinners at La Closerie des Lilas, and a few destination trips to taste Burgundies in Bourgogne and to sip Sancerre wines in the Loire, with this delightful woman beside me.

The End

www.ingramcontent.com/pod-product-compliance
Lightning Source LLC
Chambersburg PA
CBHW071249170626
46809CB00001B/144